WITHDRAWN

I WAS NEVER THE FIRST LADY

I WAS NEVER THE FIRST LADY

A Novel

WENDY GUERRA

*Translated from the Spanish
by Achy Obejas*

HarperVia

An Imprint of HarperCollins*Publishers*

I WAS NEVER THE FIRST LADY. Copyright © 2008 Wendy Guerra. English translation copyright © 2021 Achy Obejas. All rights reserved. Printed in the United States of America. No part of this book may be used or reproduced in any manner whatsoever without written permission except in the case of brief quotations embodied in critical articles and reviews. For information, address HarperCollins Publishers, 195 Broadway, New York, NY 10007.

HarperCollins books may be purchased for educational, business, or sales promotional use. For information, please email the Special Markets Department at SPsales@harpercollins.com.

Originally published as *Nunca fui primera dama* in Spain in 2008 by Ediciones B.
FIRST HARPERVIA EDITION PUBLISHED IN 2021

Designed by Bonni Leon-Berman

Library of Congress Cataloging-in-Publication Data has been applied for.

ISBN 978-0-06-299074-7

21 22 23 24 25 LSC 10 9 8 7 6 5 4 3 2 1

Thank you to Celia Sánchez's family, here and there, for their anecdotes, words, and hospitality.

To my mother, for her lost pages and recovered poetry.

To Celia, for not allowing herself to be forgotten, for soaring.

To Marco, my counsel.

To Julio Carrillo, for his style.

To the Cuban archives, to the two coasts, to all the friends who hold on to their memories.

To you, secretly.

CONTENTS

Part I

DAYBREAK WITH NO ONE

My country is that singular instant taking place right now
everywhere, the shoreline, places I don't know how
to get to, that I can't get to, and yet where I alight.

—ALBIS TORRES

E veryone's child here, reporting from a country of no one. This is Nadia Guerra, and for the first time, sitting at an open mic, I'm going to tell you what I think, what I've felt every morning of my life and during all these years when I saluted the flag and sang the national anthem. I'm going to say everything I haven't dared to say until this very moment. Listen to what I'm about to tell you here, on my radio show, live, while I take refuge in the half-light of my hermetically sealed sound booth.

I belong to that intimate place that makes me human and not divine. I'm an artist and not a contemporary heroine. I hate that lack of proportion—I don't want there to be expectations I can't meet. I don't owe the martyrs any more than I owe my parents, than I owe my own resistance, than I owe my personal history, anchored here in a simple Cuban life.

I can't keep on trying to be like Che, to inherit Camilo's purity, Maceo's courage, Agramonte's fearlessness, Mariana Grajales's fury, Martí's nomadic and creative spirit, Celia Sánchez's stoic silence. My most heroic acts are simple: to survive on this island, to avoid suicide, to deal with the guilt provoked by my obligations, to accept my good fortune of being alive, and to definitively disengage from the insistence of war and peace.

I don't want to be the martyrs' martyr, with their sagas and great epics. Standing before the heroes' statues, I've thought my death should be simple, meticulous, sober, discreet.

My true heroes are my parents, victims of their own survival, settled, drawn out, painful. Expelled from an adoring and disillusioned sect, they lost their minds.

When they looked beyond the seawall—now crumbling— they saw the sea as their only patrimony. The dark and starry bay or the luminous everyday Caribbean. But nothing could save them. They put aside their personal projects to devote themselves to collective work.

The leaders in the foreground and my parents out of focus, lost in the depth of field, far, far from the protagonists. They were endearing extras, doubles devoted to the great work, the sacred script and its complicated staging.

There were days when I felt orphaned or—I'll say it in a more conciliatory fashion—like a Child of the Nation. I saw my parents for brief periods. It wasn't personal; several friends found themselves in the same situation.

Where's your father, they'd ask.

Somewhere in Cuba, you had to say.

On how many rainy afternoons did I see grandparents from more or less normal families standing at the school door, with raincoats and umbrellas, calmly waiting. Grandfathers and grandmothers—I'd raise a monument to them myself.

I remember my parents swallowing banned words and

names while smiling for black-and-white photos. Maybe they wanted to surrender to the giant flag of lies they told—a black-and-white flag, but still a flag.

After a time, they were ambushed by their invisible enemies.

My parents weren't a part of the Revolution's triumph, because they were too young; nor did they arrive in time to enjoy the freedoms that came with such an ideal. Distressed, because they'd had no part in making the Revolution, they supported it. They held up the new society, their bodies the scaffolding. They were almost happy to take part, to be a voice in the great choir, part of the resistance. When they found themselves at the very center of that isolated generation, they were trapped; they couldn't find a way out.

But, well, my dear listeners, let's listen to some music and take a break from everything I want to confess today. Let's listen to Carlos Varela as he sings his composition "Family Portrait (*Foto de familia*)."

> *Behind all that nostalgia,*
> *all those lies and betrayals . . .*

And now, speaking about family and parents: the weight of the celebrity dead was so much greater than the lives they lived in anonymity. That's how they slowly resigned themselves to the idea that we'd be better off over there, in the humanist paradise, in that other life. How many times did we hear them say, in the middle of a meeting or in our living room or while standing in line: "It won't benefit me, no, but my daughter will have a better life."

My dears, I have news for you. I also hope for something better for my children.

This is the sound from when our parents were young, when Silvio Rodríguez and Pablo Milanés were working with the group Experimentación Sonora del ICAIC. Now let's listen to the Columna Juvenil del Centenario song, which goes like this:

> *When the sun splits in two at noon from the horror*
> *when slogans and goals beg to be killed off . . .*

It's true, no school has been named after my mother, but if I'm standing here it's because she had the nerve to write, to speak whenever she had to, and then later, when she was no longer recognized, she knew how to cry quietly, locked in a closet, smoking in the shadows between the moth-eaten coats so I wouldn't see her doubting, so she wouldn't have to lie to me with an explanation that was only more or less true about our inexplicable reality. My parents reconstructed a country within a country, just for me.

They called me Nadia, in honor of Lenin's wife. In Russian: Надежда. My name and I mean "hope."

Papá and Mamá delighted in constructing a nonexistent world, perhaps hoping to create a template for me. They made over whatever was ugly, multiplied what little we had so we could share, blurred whatever was horrible, and changed the subject so they wouldn't be cornered without a way out. That was my recurrent nightmare: that I'd be trapped in one of those popular underground tunnels, where I'd end up suffocating.

I grew up in my parents' country. By the time I arrived,

its inviolable borders were already drawn. Today I'm not so sure we all live in the same Free Territory of the Americas for which they struggled, but the country in their heads was a marvelous place. We rocked ourselves in a floating ideal, a non-place, a utopia at the very center of the Caribbean.

My mother's hands untangled unforgivable entanglements, repeated mistakes, the losses her mind couldn't conceive. She'd drown in an angry sob, fall ashamed on the battlefield, whenever she was surprised by her own lies. She was tormented because she couldn't come up with better arguments and would cough, intoxicated by nicotine and disillusionment, smearing her empty hands with salty tears. My mother ran because someone or something was stalking her. What we call the enemy was, for her, a reminder of her demons.

My dear listeners, my mother is a martyr. My father, a hero. Enough of feeling guilty over what was bestowed on us. Those we saluted from the foot of the pedestal were riddled with doubts, were prey to panic. Weren't they? Those people doubted, stepped back, disobeyed, were unfaithful or miserable; they were wrong. They divorced; they fell in love. Men and women made love standing up, with their boots on.

My parents went mute when I asked for an explanation. The heroes turned to marble when we needed them to be human. Speak, damn it! The testimony to their existence is their wives, their children and grandchildren who moved among us in school, in crowds, at summer camp, when their faces told us more about their misgivings and detachment than any speech. Together we cultivated the art of the "necessary loss." But are losses necessary?

Resignation makes it so we think it's natural to see your father's face on a huge billboard or on a political poster. Do the people share your pain, or do you share the people's pain? Do we all cry over the death of a loved one?

The children of those martyrs who grew up with me don't remember their parents either. They remember the heroes, yes, but not their parents. With their parents protected, their doubts camouflaged, it made it so I never knew much about my parents. In my more fanciful moments, I presumed I knew what they would be like in a normal state: at home, playing dominoes, sharing games.

Since we never managed to experience our parents' naiveté, since we could never be like them, who can possibly ask us— all of us—to be like the martyrs?

Every morning I pledged what I couldn't achieve: Pioneers for communism, we would be like Che. I didn't even have the nerve to just stay quiet, like my mother. I spoke and gave myself away. I expressed myself and collapsed from the guilt of not being what I was raised to be or, better, designed to be.

Maybe everything was a metaphor and not guilt. Did I ever know my parents? Did I ever know if they said yes when they wanted to say no? Will I ever know?

I continue with a campaign of pretense. I defend myself because they want to wrench something from me, to take it from me—that much I know.

Enough of this devotion to saints. I don't owe the heroes a thing. I can't swear loyalty with my hand to my forehead for even one more day of existence, because I won't be able to keep my word. Since I was a girl, I've repeated their names like an automaton: a little slogan machine dressed up like a soldier, unable to pick up even a quarter from the floor. Not arguing with the unarguable, there goes my hand, up, stiff, to my forehead. Not asking questions, because "you don't ask about what you know."

I throw flowers into the sea as I dry tears unfathomable for my age. What will Camilo think of me, given this poor bouquet? The water is carpeted with flowers, and I have brought him ten wilted carnations.

I'm dressed in someone else's clothes, olive green, patched and clean. Another Guerra uniform. I've learned to aim at an abstract target. What will be my real bull's-eye?

Do we owe everything to those heroes? Mamá and Papá, wherever you are, it looks like it was true: "Homeland or death" meant there was a chance we could die. Fall, collapse, faint. It was no metaphor, no. That we will triumph is a broad promise, marvelous and much bigger than us.

The audio engineer—I'm not going to say his name—opens his eyes and nods. He always sleeps during these hours . . .

Thank you for being with me. Even though we might not get a single call, we're here.

We've started the show today like a burst of machine-gun fire. Like certain American movies broadcast on Saturdays at midnight that set our nerves on edge. I'm the last Pioneer still awake, and I'm spending these wee hours with you. Where's your family? (Silence on the other side of the glass.)

9

Dear listeners, dear friends, I'm coming to you from an old sound booth where they used to sit my mom when the disc jockey failed to show up. In spite of the fact that she hated hearing her own voice, she was always here. She said the mics stole her soul.

I can see her. I was little, but I remember. She stood here, in front of me, next to the audio engineer, leaning on the console and smoking, the script in her hand, ready to direct the broadcast. Even though she was intimidated by having to make sense of the news, to transform it, to manipulate reality, she still had to do it. And now here we are again, with the same smell of cork and intense nicotine, broadcasting something acceptable to you on a modulated frequency.

Let's stop these ideas with a burst of machine-gun fire . . . Let's listen to some music, here on your station for life. I know, I've gone on too long, but I have this mic hanging from the sky, swaying with the perilous rhythm of my voice like a hangman's noose. As I look on, this old gadget, an RCA Victor, refuses to be silent, defies time and the enemy's abstract distance. Excuse me, aren't we used to long speeches? All my life I've gone to bed and woken listening to an oration. I can't forget the voice that haunts me. My memory wouldn't fail me.

Then let's be quiet while listening to this piece I've pulled from our musical archives . . . It's sepia, and don't forget, you heard it all on a day like today, dateless, with nothing to celebrate, right here on Radio Sun City (48.9). I'm speaking on this modulated frequency, today, right now, because tomorrow they might pull me off the air forever. But this program airs so late or so early that hardly anyone monitors it. Whoever is listening to me in these wee hours of the night *almost* agrees with me. If the censors fell asleep and failed to cut this off, then let's keep going on this nocturnal freeway . . . Then again, maybe nobody's "watching out" for us. As a friend of mine used to say, "Just because we might be psychopaths doesn't mean we're being followed." In any case, if that's how it is, let's say what we feel today; let's not leave anything unsaid. Let's breathe in this free space without guilt. Let's listen to the songs we learned for the marches or the jam sessions at the country schools, in all those empty parks in different towns, and on the steps of the university, singing in a chorus. But please, don't forget this is Radio Sun City. No, you haven't made a mistake. This is Nadia Guerra, and this is *Daybreak with No One*; we're awake for you.

We're listening to Carlos Puebla's voice, which reminds us of that song we used to sing in the camps and at school events . . .

> . . . *of your beloved presence,*
> *Comandante Che Guevara . . .*

Dear friend, let's talk like we're intimate, so we can stop behaving like we're part of the crowd and feel instead like we're complicit in something more personal. The sleep-deprived, the night owl, the lunatic, everyone who's listening to me knowing tomorrow I may not be able to divulge what I know today, what you're also thinking and don't say, just like our parents right here on this very same radio station in this city, or in one like it, when they stopped talking at this very same hour.

Let's get close . . . At this hour of the night, I can't lie to you. Listen up, my dear watchman, sleepless girl, desperate poet, citizen of a slumbering city. Do you remember this record?

You're the music I have to sing: Tony Pinelli's song in Pablo Milanés's voice.

I'd like to say what I'm feeling
on a July day in the middle of the plaza . . .

If they let us, like that old Mexican song says, we'll go on with the show. For now, only if they let us, we're going to ask ourselves some questions, the kind we usually swallow so we won't get in trouble. It's time now for interrogations.

Right this minute, dear listeners, in this very "moment of spring," almost no one will hear us. We're a club with only four or five members, bohemians, kamikazes, united by a common idea: to share our personal truths. As individuals, we need to say in singular what we think in plural.

Please call, interrogate yourselves, vent. If I'm still on the air, I'll answer. I promise. Any inveterate night owl in our secret troupe is going to be on *Daybreak with No One*.

It was and is Donato Poveda. "Like a Crystal Ball (*Como una campana de cristal*)."

Night is here with its cruel silence . . .

There have been no calls tonight. This early morning, there are no hurricanes, no strong winds to knock down the wires. It's not raining. There are no celebrations in the city, but the phone is dead. Maybe no one hears us. We'll go on.

We're going to call a forever friend—maybe she can tell us if we're on the air or not.

"Operator, please connect me with Maya's number. Let's put her on the air and see if she's listening."

"Hello."

"Abuela, sorry about the hour. Is Maya home? We want to talk to her."

"Who's this?"

"It's Nadia, Abuela. We're on the air, doing our show, and we want to know if we're being heard."

"Oh! Nadia, I was asleep, child, and I didn't recognize your voice. You sound far away. Maya left for Madrid. She didn't tell anyone. You know how discreet she is."

"Abuela, I'm sorry, I didn't know. Are you listening to my show today? We're on the air."

"What show? Maya calls on Saturdays. Come by—don't leave me alone."

"A kiss from our sound booth, Abuela. Of course I'll come by. Ciao."

"A sound booth here or there? Where are you, child?"

"Sweet dreams, Abuela."

Maya, another one who left without saying goodbye. We'll go on. If anyone can hear us, please call.

In 1979, when I was nine, Silvio Rodríguez wrote this love song I can't forget. Let's listen to it.

Today my duty was
to sing to the homeland . . .

I'd like to tell you how I got here. It's been six months since we began broadcasting this show, and I've never confessed, because someone like me, who comes from the world of visual art, with exhibits and performances, who is afraid of being ridiculous, afraid of the night's frailties and decadence, terrified of catchphrases, of the old ways of communicating . . . Why do I—someone without habits or traditions, not dependent on any ritual—come here every day to be with you?

My mother was a brain, a voice. Twenty years ago she had a program at this station: *Words Against Forgetting*. She recorded some gorgeous songs; she preserved lost voices, voices that had already died in our memories but were still alive in the country's culture. My mother did all she could to preserve a phenomenon as big as old Cuban music, what we know today as the Buena Vista Social Club. But she disappeared. Maybe she listens to me from an old lighthouse on a lost beach. Mami, are you listening?

Maybe it's better if we listen to some of the old scratchy recordings she didn't forget to leave behind, like this one, which she saved before leaving forever.

Don't fall asleep, and if you do, dream of us. This sounds better all the time . . . It's the great Barbarito Díez singing about absence in these wee hours of the night when it seems no one is tuned in to us.

Absence means forgetting,
means shadows, means never . . .

That's why it's now my turn to stand guard with you in these early mornings, no matter how ridiculous or marvelous it may seem. They're our secret and, at the same time, our small oeuvre. Coming back here is like coming back to my mother.

This discourse is like a matryoshka inside another matryoshka. It's also like the guffaw from those who sang me to sleep with prayers and what one friend called "our communist pamphlet." I've been educated in such a way that no matter how much I may reject the lessons, they haunt me like a stigma, an attitude toward life, toward justice and destiny. Truths, lies. No matter my expression, it's obvious how I was built, structured for others. Abstract but real. However they could, along the way. That's how I am, how so many of us are—we're contaminated. To deny it makes us cynical, dishonest, crafty, alienated. Or did we kill my mother and that's why I'm here, playing with her cards against forgetting?

I have a sense no one's listening to us today. The phone hasn't rung all night. The audio engineer and I have been alone here, separated by only greenish glass (from the 1950s), sharp and cold, like this booth. Waiting for a response from the other side of the hermetic city, patched up, marked by its past. Tomorrow, the day after tomorrow, or Monday, I'll be with you. You'll listen to me, lying down or wandering around the house, around the empty factory or as it's about to open, around the abandoned movie house you take care of as it slowly crumbles in solitude, or maybe you're listening to me while in a taxi no one can ride in because by now everyone's home or not out yet . . . It doesn't matter. Tomorrow we'll still be *Daybreak with No One*. You can go to sleep with me now. Until tomorrow, I'll leave you with this marvelous *guaguancó* in Celeste Mendoza's voice:

> *If I lose your love,*
> *it won't matter much.*

NOTES FROM MY DIARY

Of course they canceled my show, but no one expected anything different.

It's all part of the game. I'm interested only in the finite. I'm a professional provocateur.

They heard rumors; at that hour, everyone's sleeping. It looks like my suspension is for one month. The mystery continues: "Victory is certain." I've applied for two grants. If I get one, I won't be able to keep coming to the radio station every day. I've thought about building a studio at home, something artisanal where I can even record noise.

The exhibit at Reina Sofía in Madrid, even though it included a boatload of other artists, was much talked about. I'm still part of Everyone, never a protagonist. Once more, my individuality hurts, narrows, and flows like a river trying to map its course. The critics talk about the White Library I've built, a flawless space filled with books, papers, documents, spines, flaps—all white, unblemished. It's ready for reading, ready to inform, but there's nothing there. Saúl talks about this exercise in literary silence: Is nothing really written or, on the contrary, is it a staging of the Literature of Nothing? Does the existence of a typology—a library—in and of itself guarantee access to its content? Or, rather, does every predetermined structure censor the possibility of generating a free and subjective experience?

They come to interview me and leave with something in their hands or on their tape recorders. They try to manipulate things, but I don't know anymore who manipulates whom. I had control once, but the steering wheel's come off since then.

Havana's humid cold is upon us. The sea splatters my window with salt; the drizzle cuts right through to the bone. I inhale, exhale; I look out the window. Inhaling ideas into my stuffed-up head, but it's contaminated by egos, so the ideas won't work. With each passing day I see the real world less clearly. Everything is hazy, wet from rain, and looks like something pulled out of a painting by Gustavo Acosta.

My work is exhibited far away. I'm part of all that, but I won't move; my work travels for me. Goodbye, White and Black flags! Goodbye, White Library!

The radio show is my work too; it's been my best work these last few months. I wanted to expose myself to the quotidian life of the nighttime programs. Wherever we are in the world, we're assailed by the mournful voice of the speaker in a kind of neuro-vaginal tone as we doze.

When I couldn't resist anymore, when its anachronistic aesthetic began to suffocate me, I blew it up with truths in a place where truth can be a bomb. I launched the show at dawn, as if I was free to say what I wanted with my own mouth, but I knew there were consequences. As someone who covers a canvas following orders from someone else, or axes her favorite sculpture to pieces. That's how I got firewood from my fallen tree. We all know how far we can go, where the limits are on a modulated frequency. The radio plagues me, between cars, windows, parks, on buses running their routes. There's a news story, a song, a sound in my head. Asleep or awake, I hear voices from the radio. We're not dumb, dear listeners; we know how far we can go when we say "Wow."

For the time being, I'll stop broadcasting for "others" and begin exclusive transmissions I can later give as gifts to my friends. Homemade broadcasts, alternatives. I'll fill my radio shows with songs and commentaries as personal as the entries in my diary. I'll do a program with my own ideas and music. No one can censor my autonomy. It's not that I want to broadcast but that I want to express myself. That's how it's going to be from now on. I don't want to give up the radio because it's part of me. But the radio can give up on me, at least given these grave circumstances to which I've made myself vulnerable.

I was born somewhere between radio and film. That's me: sound and image; rebellious, tropical; socialist, surrealist, hyperrealist. Special effects are a kind of Dadaism that transports and defines the limits of any body and the sounds inside my sick head.

NOTE

Two pieces really had an effect on me at Documenta in Kassel. In the same show in which Tania Bruguera created a mirage in which you entered a dark tunnel and then were dazzled by a light and the only sounds you could hear were machine guns and boots marching, I also discovered a piece by a Jewish artist in which she'd

reconstructed and compiled facts about her mother in
a concentration camp. She'd never known she was part
of a persecuted family. After many years, she'd found
a numbered plate among her mother's belongings and
decided to investigate, to shed light on the lives of her
parents.

In fact, I don't know if my mother's still alive. We know
she had Alzheimer's. Someone witnessed her being out of
her mind, but so much time has passed since then, we assume she must be dead. It's better like this, after so much
absence. I hate having to arrange my affections so it's only
by killing someone off that I can save them from their own
existence, from their great miseries and mistakes. Maybe I'll
find her. For my father, it's best to drop the subject, to assume
my mother is lost. He doesn't have any excuses anymore. He
doesn't have anything good or bad to tell me about her anymore. In his own way, my father is also dying. He doesn't
have secrets.

Does anyone know where she is? Does anyone know why
they give my father so many homages? At this point, why
do they keep going over something that's sealed and silent?
Why do they keep pointing something out they used to con-
sider off-limits: Hands off! Don't touch!

Many mysteries. This could be my next solo show: The
search and rescue of my mother. My father's final act.

I've received another letter from a listener who usually writes
to me in care of the station.

His name is Eduardo, and he's been a fan since the begin-

ning of the show from which I've been temporarily suspended.
I attach it to my diary because, though it hurts, he's still right.

Dear Comrade Guerra:
I feel terrible about the void your program has left us
with, your "lunatic" listeners. Believe me, we've missed
you these days. For my family and me, it's as if we've
been abandoned by someone we hold very dear.
     The truth is, we need it every night as an incentive
because of our many personal deprivations. By
this I mean transportation, money squandered for
entertainment, et cetera, although I don't believe
anything in life is eternal.
     My wife's and my point about your departure from the
show is that, really, you were a little irresponsible when
you exposed yourself like that. Didn't you realize you
were playing with fire? How much of your discourse was
really naive, playing the naughty girl while working at a
place like that? That lack of responsibility is related to the
abandonment with which you accuse your parents. You've
also left us to ourselves. So please respect our rights as
parents to abandon ship in turn. Here we're all guilty
of abandonment. I hope we can agree on that. Don't be
offended and try to understand it as a life lesson.
                                        Best wishes,
                                        Eduardo and family

Eduardo and his family's letter is clear. It's not the first
time he's counseled me with that paternal tone, as if he sees

everything about to happen and stops it. I don't know who he is, but every time I've gotten in trouble, he seems to have seen it coming. Cuban paternalism has no limits. They take it seriously. They write to you even though they don't know you. Maybe my friend the listener has gone through all this. I don't know. It's another one of those mysteries with which we live.

I wonder who these people are who take the time to call a radio station, to write to shows and worry about those on the other side. My friend the listener makes me very curious.

I remember one night when I was a girl, a man was waiting for my mother at the reception desk of the station where she worked. He had a VEF radio in his hands, Russian, heavy and black. He wanted my mother—specifically her—to pull the station out of it. He didn't want to hear it coming out of that radio anymore.

We were dismayed. Someone said he was abnormal. As far as I was concerned, he was brave, a crazy man who dared say what others kept quiet.

Get this station out of my radio! I can't take it anymore, comrade, I can't take it . . . !

At least he was looking for an irreversible solution, not just moving the dial from right to left.

I'm still putting my homemade show together. I have to go to the station for an urgent meeting, which I think might be definitive.

MEETING AT THE STATION

The moment I stepped out of the elevator, I looked toward the director's office and saw my audio engineer coming out and looking like a scolded puppy. He kissed me, his eyes watering, and said goodbye. Was this a definitive farewell? It could be—I wouldn't be surprised. I'm so irresponsible. And I started to blame myself.

I waited, as if I were back in school outside the principal's office.

I didn't know what the hell we were waiting for. Edelsa sat at her big black "Spanish regret"–style desk. She stared at me as if she were the school principal, but instead of scolding me, she started doodling a beard, mustache, and glasses on a picture in an old sepia-toned newspaper. I was disgusted to see that the top of her blue pen was chewed up. Didn't she want to talk? Wasn't she going to talk at all this morning? Why had she asked to see me, then? Finally, a "comrade" she had been waiting for arrived. Edelsa came to like a domestic robot. She threw the newspaper into the trash, and right then I realized the face she'd been doodling belonged to Captain San Luis. Oh, oh, oh. What madness!

In contrast, the "comrade" arrived radiating happiness, sweaty and ready to chat.

He tousled my hair.

"So, little girl, what's up with us now?"

Oh, everything's plural here, a kind of modest plural.

"Nothing, nothing's up with us," I said, my voice as firm as a soldier's, afraid of what might happen but still firm.

Edelsa rolled her eyes. It was strange: she looked behind her, to the sides, and laughed ironically. They sat face-to-face, and Edelsa launched into a speech that seemed preprogrammed.

"The word is 'suicidal.' I told you maybe it's a biological problem; her mother had disorders. Since her training days we've helped her a great deal. They're very similar, so I won't blame the girl. What we, the counselors, suggest is that perhaps she can get help at the military clinic, so she'll see how things are."

All of this was said in front of me without a thought to being discreet. As if I didn't exist. I thought the idea was to scare me; I couldn't think of why else they'd do that. I didn't want to find out about my mother like this. My God!

The "comrade" stared right at me. He emptied the ashtray into a trash can that was already full and then stepped out for something. Edelsa and I stayed behind, trapped and mute.

In my mother's defense, I tried to tell Edelsa something about her, but Edelsa just made this noise: *Shhhhhhhhhhhh-hhh.* She pointed to the curtains or the ceiling—I'm not sure which—and opened her eyes wide. We fell into a deep silence.

I didn't say a word for six or eight minutes—for me, an eternity. I surveyed the office: the curtains a dirty mustard color, plaster busts of unknown martyrs, several marble trophies, and tin badges a little corroded by time. Fake RCA mics and, especially, books in perfect Russian, which I imagined dealt with radio policies, thoughts about art and socialism, Spanish–Russian dictionaries, and vice versa. That's when I remembered Edelsa had a degree in community communications from the Soviet Union. My father once told me it was Edelsa who'd had the idea of presenting Russian language classes on the radio. Anyway, I was still exploring the shelves, with their dusty matryoshkas and photographs. There she was, a Cuban mulatta between bridges and monuments buried in snow, wearing a ushanka, smiling in pictures all over the office. Everything was suspended in time, frozen on a Siberian steppe, the AC on max and Russian postcards on top of the icebox in order of size. The icebox was Soviet too, and not well taken care of, but still working. I doubted Russian bureaucrats kept a similar setup in their country. This was untouchable. It was loyal to what no longer existed, a second opportunity.

Finally our man was at the door. Edelsa tried to hurry him.

"Lázaro, we need to talk to the Party to take care of . . . that other thing. But let's take care of this once and for all."

She turned down the cold coffee he offered her in a paper cup. I didn't want any either.

"You have two options, he said. Either you go and get tested and do whatever the psychiatrist tells you to do, so you're calmer, more measured, in control of yourself, or we'll let you go for medical reasons."

Edelsa looked at him, a bit confused.

"But, Lazarito, if she doesn't go to the doctor, how can she be let go from here for medical reasons? I'm unclear about that."

I stood up, took Lázaro's hand, and shook it. Finally the person assigned to watch me had a name. I asked for some blank paper, in fact a few recycled pages with old scripts written on the back. Edelsa was confused but gave them to me. I took her blue pen from her mouth, gnawed and wet. While they looked on in a thick and almost lucid silence, I left my unmistakable mark. I wrote while standing, using clear print: "I'm leaving voluntarily because I don't feel capable of doing this job in the way that's being asked of me." I signed it: "Nadia Guerra."

Edelsa and Lázaro read it. It was exactly what they didn't want.

There was already a form letter for resignations, a methylene-blue stencil. An act of conscience. Lázaro looked over at Edelsa, who quickly crumpled my note, then tore it to pieces.

"Child, there's a way of doing things, a process." She handed me a gray form. "This is the official letter of resignation, if you don't want to accept going to the clinic. Of course, we hope you'll go; we don't want to lose you. Young people are shaped, not abandoned." She put the form letter in my hand: murky, watered down, illegible. I couldn't deal with it. I didn't even want to think about what they were asking me to sign.

Lázaro asked Edelsa if I'd been warned by the Party representative at the station or by the creative division or by the station employees themselves.

"It's not a question of paternalism, but young people have to be helped along. They're not born knowing, Edelsa. I don't believe genetics are irreversible; people can be educated. This is a failure of the institutions."

Lázaro looked me straight in the eye without hesitation. I returned his gaze, grateful for the gesture. This is what we've come down to. There are so few people who will look you in the eye.

They talked about my genetics as if they were referring to the locker where I kept my audiotapes. What is this?

"Little compañera Guerra, has a colleague or a friend or even a listener approached you to warn you about the practical aspects of this job?"

"No," I said, playing the victim.

"Are you sure, little compañera? No one, no one in or out of the station, has warned you about this kind of excess in the medium?"

"No one," I said, embarrassed. I felt like I was in grammar school again. I hate being scolded.

"She's suicidal, like her mother," said Edelsa between gritted teeth.

"Well, it seems to me more like collective murder than a suicide because it hurts everyone, because you can't just go on the air from your own home. Nadia, we're the state and we're responsible for what people are told. We have to be very thoughtful about what we say to the people. Frankly, my dear, improvising your talks, talking to the four winds as if the station were yours, that could have really hurt the station if it'd been heard. It would have hurt you even more than the station: you wouldn't have been able to travel; they wouldn't have let you get your mouth near a mic for another twenty years. Thanks to our constant vigilance, we don't broadcast those kinds of disorganized or hysterical thoughts. That's an improper act by a child of the Revolution, who is who she is because of the Revolution, who owes everything she is to the Revolution. Very brave on your part, but very off base for the leadership here. Who would you please with these immature acts? The enemy. Your friends would applaud you, but you're not going to go down in

27

history because of these tantrums. We don't deserve this, Nadia. We've been very tolerant with you and your family."

I don't know why but I kissed them, I kissed them both very quickly, just to get it over with, and I went running like a naughty girl, leaving the door open, and leaving—in the worst hands—my signature's incoherent line. It was a document I'd regret signing, but I considered it part of the collection in my personal museum.

This is all for today, my dear friends. Until next time.

NOTE

I'm not going to resign from my radio program. I don't know what life is like without being on the air. I'm doing this for me and for those who want to listen to me.

WRITING IN MY DIARY

Two days later, I take up the task of structuring *An Hour with No One*. This is my new piece, a new program to give my private life to my friends. Mouth to mouth . . . real life and music I've burned on CDs. This is my new movement. *An Hour with No One* will be *Nadia's Hour*, the most transparent program that never existed. A show recorded on my computer, in my house, and distributed to my friends. I'm here, working on this idea. Ideas exist so long as we give them life; when they're inside us . . . they disappear. "What's not named ceases to exist."

Black tufts of hair on the white floor. Wisps of fine straight hair fall like grass at my bare feet. Dark streaks and then a drop of blue, red, ultraviolet blood spreads on the checkered floor in the living room. Now a scream in the air and the doorbell, shattering our little intimacy. We've cut the phone line and thus cut off the outside world.

"Child, don't move—I cut my finger!"

Since I was a kid, my father has cut my hair. I would never let my hair grow long. He didn't have the patience for braids, even less when it came to dealing with the lice I picked up at school. The sound of the scissors at my ears, me choking from the cigarette smoke, loose words—that was my life. My dad is my hairdresser, my counselor, my nurse, my cook. My father is me.

It's a few hours before the opening of the Latin American Film Festival, before the homage he'll receive, a kind of eulogy in life to try to ease the pain they've caused him. We talk between snips of the scissors and the cologne, talcum powder, the little electric shaver, nail polish, makeup, scripts full of scribbles, and ash on the dining table.

My dad's famous, respected by the elite, adored by his students, and attacked since the '60s for everything he's dared to say. Dear Diary, you know that—you wouldn't let me lie.

And who am I? I'm my father's daughter. He's the rock in my shoe. My pointer, my scratched record, my nightmare. Everywhere else in this world my father's on duty, on billboards, in magazines and on the banners announcing his retrospectives, in the words my friends quote from his scripts. There are hit records with theme songs from his films. My father is a great film director; he's a one-man orchestra. He's the myth that blurs the mirrors because wherever he goes it's impossible to see anything else. My father was around in the '60s, '70s, '80s, '90s, and he'll be there in the 2000s because they can't do anything to silence him. He's a nonconformist, and talented. As far as I'm concerned, no other man can compare. So I go to the psychiatrist and we start with the Oedipus complex. Not that I think it's relevant, but others believe it matters. They wear me out looking where there's nothing to see, and avoiding looking where there might be something they're afraid to find.

I got the two grants I applied for, one in France and the other in the United States. I'm a grants hunter and I shoot every which way. I'd always been turned down before, but now there's a chorus saying yes! No one believes I deserve any of it.

Patiently, my father has been cutting my hair for the last thirty years.

"Papi, I applied for two grants and I got them both, but people think it's because of you."

"It's because of you. You have my brains, my name, and now you have yourself."

I am desperate by the time I arrive at the opening. I can be delusional and self-referential. People are always looking for the least important details, gossiping. Undoubtedly, they will say: "She's Daddy's girl. She gets her daddy's leftovers."

I've made a decision. I won't use this grant for what I said in my application. To hell with Atelier Calder, to hell with the Guggenheim, to hell with research, to hell with everything. I'm Nadia. I'm going to look for my mother. I'm nobody, nothing, and I need to know who the rest of me is.

JANUARY 1, 2006, 7:30 A.M.

Havana on January 1st seems like the Sahara surrounded by water. Dust, rocks, and silence. The blue background goes unnoticed and saves us.

I don't know much about dawn in other places. At this hour, on a day like today, I go swimming in the Caribbean. I want the sea to wash me clean of all the negativity I carry in my head and my body. "The sea doesn't fit inside anyone's head." Here, on January 1st, we commemorate everything and celebrate nothing. On January 1st at this hour, the triumph of the Revolution is on display. Flags and whatnots hang from the balconies alongside wet laundry. The street seems like an ice rink without ice, it's so empty. There's not a single car braking on the avenues. Everything's dormant.

I now have all the plans for what I'm going to burn in the gardens at Atelier Calder in France. My sculptures are heroes made of fire and ice. They may melt or go up in flames, but those are my heroes.

I'm told the grounds at the Château de Saché are snowed in.

I'll make two sculptures a day: one from fire and one from ice.

The one from fire: a great sculpture, human-size, made from leaves and clothes, which will be burned. Lit every night against the white background, it'll look fabulous. That's the hero who wears my father's face.

The one from ice: a similar sculpture, carved out of snow, built on wires shaped into the body of a heroine with my mother's face.

From ice to water, from fire to a frozen cold. One burns, one melts.

I'm a pyromaniac, and I'm fascinated by burning everything. It must be because I was raised between blackouts.

I'm going to immortalize my father and search for my mother. It's an ephemeral but personal gesture. It's my nighttime ritual in Atelier Calder's snow. These are the heroes for my altar of fire and ice on the feeble frost of my body, where the water melts and eases away from me.

Second idea: the fire figure will be a guerrilla. Like one of those wax sculptures. I'm thinking about the Museum of the Revolution. Materials: leaves, wool, wire, military boots, cap, olive-green uniform. She'll have the face of a well-known guerrilla, and on close inspection the face will reveal itself clearly as my mother's, a beloved stranger who burns and dies.

My dad's asleep on the couch. I'm going to Paris tomorrow and I'll miss home, I'll miss Cuba, I'll miss myself. I'm going to go swimming. Dear Diary: Happy New Year.

PACKING MY BAGS AND TAKING
THE ISLAND WITH ME

I PUT your broken dragonfly at the bottom of my empty suitcase. Then blankets and socks for this absurdly cold weather spring.

I know they'll read my diaries, but I take them with me anyway. They'll take my things, go through my underwear.

Ah! To ask permission in order to render myself nude in my drawings. There they are, the drawings, snuck into my life's suitcase. Me, in my glassy tears. Screens full of doubts, backlit by the desire rooted in this eternal journey.

The songs of my generation, screaming our fears, faking them. The excess weight of hidden ideas, things I don't want to declare. All of this terrifies me.

Books by dead authors in order to survive.

Books by living authors I miss when I read them and whose hands I feel on the wet paper.

Originals, anchors, seaweed—they all help me escape this drowning feeling.

At the very bottom, some mottled mangos from Pinar del Río, contraband: their smell will give me away.

Sand from the beach at Santa María, rum from Santiago, and a Virgin, who'll keep me from hurting when I touch bottom.

Wings flapping, the broken dragonfly takes off; this tousle-haired Cuban girl's trying to stuff the island in her suitcase.

Winter clothes, bathing suits for the sun.

An endless journey with this bottomless suitcase.

JANUARY 2, 2006
(RED DIARY)

At the Havana airport, tears fall like scattered pearls to the floor, the "marble of farewells." I slip and fall, without fail.

Planes. People saying "See you later." My father standing at attention like a soldier; my father saying goodbye until I don't know when. Now I remember his crazy story about my dramatic inclination toward weeping. That early morning when I wouldn't stop crying: He grew desperate. My mother had walked out the door, I was five months old, and it was just Papi and me, alone together. He tried to give me a bottle. Tried giving me drops for colic. Rocking me at top speed in the living room rocking chair. He would lay me down and pick me up without success. Until, finally, terrified, he offered me his nipple, and that's when this man that is my father (thirty years younger then) noticed I had begun to fall asleep.

My mother returned later, but only to leave us forever when I was ten years old. In 1980, she fled from Cuba. We've never known why, or at least no one's ever told me. Weaned (from her), already used to my father's arms, I almost didn't miss her, and we went on with our lives together.

"Goodbye, goodbye, see you soon."

I cry quietly as the customs agents check my books, my papers, ask me questions that have no answers. Routine will bring order to this. I think of my father and I remember that piece: "A Stop on the Way to Egypt." The agent asks me many questions and I gift him with two pearls from my eyes, made in Cuba.

Tired of saying goodbye, my father goes home. I remain in limbo, between Cuba and the World. "Territorial Waters," Island, Father, Goodbye.

A month to get to know him, five minutes to undress him. An hour to wake him.

I think about Marguerite Yourcenar's quote about disliking watching loved ones while they slept—how they were getting away from her more so than taking a break.

When I saw Saúl arrive, suitcase in hand, I locked myself in the bathroom so I wouldn't have to greet him. I didn't want to talk to him. We were introduced and I ran off. Although the excuse for these grants is a search for my mother, I stuck my hand in my coat pocket and pulled out a photo of my father.

Saúl looks like my dad. My psychiatrist would lift my punishment. It's no longer a subconscious fact; I pursue my father even in bed. My father in another body, my father in me. I told Saúl while he was making his wooden pieces. He'll end up as a critic and curator; his mind gets in the way of the beautiful art he could make. The force of his intelligence kills the results.

Piano keys on a grand scale. Earth and snow at once. Saúl isn't scared off. He gets it, all of it. He shaved his head with a gadget that looks like a little lawnmower. Saúl watches as I create my parents; he knows they'll vanish soon. Ephemeral art. To kill one's parents, said the judgmental psychiatrist. For the moment, I shave off what little hair's left on Saúl's head with the gadget.

We make love with the same precision with which his chisel tears at the edges of the wood. It's much more beautiful to watch him undress than to see me throw my clothes on the floor. He undresses perfectly, like a woman. He understands the codes for posing nude. Five minutes later and we're inside each other. Saúl and I, not knowing each other, trapped in the snows of Saché. He pummels me over the wood and I like it; my desire is such that I begin to cry; the secret honey from my body empties into Saúl's mouth. I open my legs like a port and let the lights pass under the bridges. Hunger and thirst. Hunger and fear. Saúl seems Cuban, but he's not. He smells of oysters when he sleeps, and I dive down to quaff at his sex, to swallow him, curl into him, lost in his carelessness, moaning.

With Saúl, the truth is a lie. Women from all over the world call him here, while he's at this atelier in the middle of nowhere in France. There are emails in many languages. Saúl doesn't tell me he loves me. I make up Saúl's love. I make him lie, I help him lie, I give him the tools to lie. He says he holds me in esteem and that he's alone. He doesn't know my country or my father or my house, none of my absurd pedigree. He knows nothing of the men whose lives I've been a part of.

The women he embodies continue on the telephone and in his smell. Saúl lies and I let him hurt me, hurt me with his mute sword, until he drowns in the pain of having hurt me.

Here, "as you can see on the laminated page," Saúl conducts private interventions in my soul. Not knowing who we are, Saúl and I make art in the snow. Spells in the white stuff. White magic.

I call my house before waking Saúl. There's so much snow, the door's blocked. I want to tell my dad I met Saúl, I've seen snow. It's me who answers in Havana, Cuba, 537.

"Hello. Papi and I are out for a while. Leave your message and I'll surely get back to you." Beeeeep.

Surely? I can surely call myself? What would I tell me? I don't know. I have nothing new to tell me. Same old thing, same as always: that I want to find my mother.

"Saúl, wake up. The snow has us trapped and I'm Cuban. I'm going to freeze; get me out of here. I want to see the sun, I want the sea."

"I hate the sea," says a sleeping Saúl, leaving me alone in that distant atelier in the middle of nowhere in France.

FEBRUARY 20, 2006, PARIS

Saúl taught me to ski. We fashioned our skis from two royal palm leaves a Dominican artist left behind. We reinforced them with resin so they were both firm and light. We used feathers to keep warm and fly through this harsh winter blast. Like a blade on the wind, we sliced through the landscape, made tracks on the snow as we slid down the nearby hills. I went from my hidden peak to the fiery frost of his sex. "Eskimo word." I like this man; I could love him if he didn't lie. The truth is his sex is dark, Mediterranean, strong, impulsive like the outgoing tide as it grapples with the rocks on the shore, tearing at the seaweed, shattering driftwood. The truth is this slender Cuban girl fused with this Catalonian, as sinewy as ebony, illuminated like the Ancients. At three in the morning he talks about Kant as if he's talking about himself. I talk about hurricanes as we watch the snow fall. We both levitate. Yes, that's it, the Mediterranean versus the Caribbean in the midst of a hurricane that this solitary island must defend against. A lost island that wanted to swallow the fierce, scheming, masculine Mare Nostrum, cultured and extravagant. A sage sea, a sea that bumps against my thighs, pulling me down with his wise words. What kind of sex is this? Depressive sex, succulent sex, sex infused by Barthes, Beckett, Derrida,

Musil. My God, there are so many people in this bed! I don't understand; I just touch. I walk his back with my fingers and revel in desire down to the tips of my toes. I feel water on my thighs. Heat, pain, a spray of semen, which gives itself away on tasting. It's snow and mango.

RED DIARY

Saúl is that cautious ship, suspicious even of what his eyes see, an awkward freighter testing the waters without the aid of any small tugboats, shipwrecked in his own high style, thrown by unprecedented tales that are elevated by his soulless telling. There's a cautious architecture to his achievements, a fearful structure to his foretelling. No one asks for anything more than a bit of fealty in the moment of intimacy. The rest is out there, gusting against our door. A list of women's names comes down the chimney, secretly whispering their longings to this talking head.

We made love one and one thousand times on this snow that's nothing more than sand at Varadero, smelling like new. We made love outside, while my sculptures blazed over white nights in Saché.

My body: I always bleed the first time. Surrender is never free; I leave something behind in exchange for the love I brew inside me. I break one umbilical cord and tie myself tight to another. Three red drops brighten the ice. It's beautiful to see them expand at my feet. Saúl steps on the purple pool; he hadn't noticed the composition. You hurt and re-member, you hurt and forget.

As he speaks in Catalan about his theories on fatigue, Saúl cooks the cod.

Everything smells of shellfish even though we're far from the coast. It smells of shellfish because of our sex, mixed with dead fish and topics as spicy as Derrida, Eco, Barthes, ufff; now I understand why he's interested in the concept of fatigue. I thought by leaving Cuba I would have escaped all that pedantry. "The Richness of the Inner World." I'm terri-fied of quoting anything. Saúl is forty-five years old and run-ning away. "Because of his misadventures, his soul is deep and dark." He likes music only in English. He doesn't under-stand my fondness for music in Spanish. He strongly defends his mother tongue but never uses it to write or express him-self. I ask him to let me listen to something in Catalan. We make a trade. He takes out *Llibre d'amic* by Joan Vinyoli, love poems, from the bottom of his suitcase. In exchange he asks that I read the interview with Derrida called "I Can't Write Without Artificial Light."

If he's doing this to bug me, he's succeeded. I went through university and half my studies in Havana reading *without artificial light*. Wicks, candles, Chinese lanterns, kerosene lamps . . . or the sun itself—whatever would illuminate and help me with my assignments and finishing my work. I tell him what it's cost me to come this far, studying, living with-out artificial light, but he doesn't understand. I try not to feel at a disadvantage. He would rather ignore everything that's a narrative of my previous world. Whatever I've been before we met isn't important to him. I couldn't be more wrecked; I feel the heel of his shoe grinding his ideas into my head. I come from a third world radiant with natural light. I can work in any circumstance.

How many times were we left in the dark in those radio sound booths, with that deathly silence, that silence as if the studio had been isolated, muzzled.

Central Havana. A little past Trillo Park, my classmate Carlos del Puerto (Jr.) sits next to a huge propane light and practices the bass at the front door of his house. The bow tearing away, sounding out the chord in the dark, his hair loose, wet, the whole neighborhood in shadows, and that instrument bellowing, wailing in the dead of night.

Don't you write by artificial light?

Cubans don't live without artificial problems. I don't understand them and they don't understand me.

Saúl gives me texts to read that complicate the conversation at an ethical, referential level. He talks about art; I talk about real life. "You come from a fertile world," he says, adding that Europe strikes him as fatigued. He has exhausted his need to teach me, as if I were a disorderly and tribal creature.

Our conversation doesn't really exist; we're like a mute talking in signs to a blind man. I swallow the cod in silence; there's light, but I feel the same anguish as I do during the damned blackouts. Artificial light won't do Saúl any good.

If we didn't write without artificial light, half of Cuban

literature wouldn't exist. My respects to Derrida, but for Saúl, indifference. Why doesn't he want to understand where I'm from? Why does his heavy intelligence, his thick cast-iron culture, ruin our desire, love, the joy of our meeting? He's lifeless.

In the meantime, let's enjoy his crispy fish in red wine, as substantial as his voice, as dark as his sex.

"Other tastes, Cuban girl, other textures, a bit of the world in your mouth . . . Stop talking and swallow."

He spreads tomato sauce on bread as if he were rubbing my thighs. He gets his round fingers messy; his thin elbows flap crazily in the night air; the wine transports us; my mouth becomes water; red upon red, earth and salt. Saúl pà amb tomàquet.

It's like in Havana, when everything's turned on and madness strikes: the lights are back!

ESKIMO WORD

For you, I'll leave the snow and ski on sand; I won't write graffiti on the snow; I'll have a Western accent and summer clothes; my teeth won't sink into any skin but yours; my smell will dissolve in your lavender water; just like the sturgeon loses its roe, I'll lose my name; I'll forget the rituals of the igloo, the woman, and the prisoner; I'll look at the melting ice as if it were water from my sex; I won't give to strangers what belongs to you at the end of the night; I'll stay in your bed dodging the fire; I'll keep the bait and the fish from my mouth; I'll free the dogs from the sled; I'll try to forget the exile from ice; we'll winter together as long as winter hurts.

On the edge of the iceberg as we travel on this white island, my mother's tears and my father's pleading whispers echo, because even if it's just a dream, we sleep on a Japanese futon on the floor and he's up in years, his body aches. I ask myself: "Nadia, what are you doing here? Who are you waiting for? Run, Nadia, run!"

I'm asleep and trying to run, but something trips up my feet, and I can't help but wake Saúl. Saúl hates to be woken and sleeps with earplugs.

"*Es quan dormo que hi veig clar.*"

I don't understand a thing. I suppose he means he's not

sleeping like he should, but I don't know. When he's asleep, he resorts to Catalan, and speaking his language makes him more beautiful and virile, but a man who sleeps with earplugs is not a very sexy sight.

I get up, walk around the house. I ask myself what it would be like to live in exile. I'm terrified of not being able to go back. Of not being able to mop the floor tiles of that house and walk barefoot, my house in Havana. Where's my father now? My father and his mysteries, my father and his films.

He's sick, like an old wolf, and I can only lick his wounds. He doesn't want to interrupt his daughter. He waits for death with dignity, exactly as he'd hoped, day after day, sitting on his laurels. He doesn't say so, but he's dreamed of a theater jampacked with people who rise to applaud his work through the very last reel.

I'm my father, but with the body and gestures of a woman.

I've been denied a visa to the United States. For the time being, I won't be able to use my Guggenheim.

Change of plans. I call my mother's friends. I want to find her. I review the clues. No one says anything coherent about her. They seem to have forgotten her; they're all different people now.

Saúl has finished his residency. He lies and lies and says he's just going on vacation to Formentera, and he does, but with a woman with whom he swims naked, forgets everything. Saúl keeps lying after saying he's sorry, and he keeps surfing the internet to find a match. Who the devil is Saúl? Where's my mother?

I call Saúl to complain about the visa denied. I tell him I'm leaving Cuba on a raft and that I'll take photos as we get closer to Florida. Saúl says we Cubans use our problems to get what we want: success, galleries, press, notoriety.

I've spent the morning crying about his insult. In my head, I review the art made in Spain and France during the worst periods of the war.

Saúl didn't dare say *Guernica* is an invention to garner success. No one would say such a thing. Because of the distance, hard times give way to hard reactions. Goodbye, Saúl.

I find some of my mother's friends, but few believe I'll

have any luck; she's a disaster. She's changed addresses eleven times in eight years. I gather letters to and from my mother's friends. For those who don't want to be signatories, I add a copyright symbol in my diary.

Dear loved ones,
I don't know how but I finally and urgently need to find my mother. Any detail could be of interest to me. I'm in Paris—communication is much easier here. Please let me know when and where you last saw her. The smallest detail could lead me to her. I'm enclosing my postal and email addresses. Kisses from the cold.

Please think about this and pass this email on to anyone who could give me some news. I'm grateful and love you all very much.

Nadia

P.S. Any information . . .

Skinny girl:
I've only seen your mother that time I told you about, in Mexico when she was crossing the street and took off like a rocket when she saw me. I was at the entrance to my hotel with two friends waiting for a ride to take us to the sound check. In fact, I've always wondered if it was really her because she looked exactly the same. If I've kept quiet about certain things from the past, it's been for everyone's benefit; please don't have any doubts

about my intentions. Whatever you can do to find her,
you should do now. You can certainly count on me.

DR

Nadia:

When we were kids and our parents were lovers and
met in secret, I only had eyes for you. I don't remember
your mother much. A pair of perfect legs would cross the
living room to my father's room, then they'd appear later
and drag you out to the sidewalk. I'll ask him if he has
any news about the woman who broke him in two.

I'm still in Mexico, and on TV. Sports. In spite of all your
prognostications, I haven't married and I don't have children.

I love you.

Diego

To your mother's daughter:

I acknowledge receipt of your letter.

She and I said goodbye at Funeraria Park in February
1969. Remember that, like La Avellaneda, I was one of
the first to leave. That jewel of a woman was already
going out with that ugly and skinny man who shall
remain unnamed and who is now so famous on our
beautiful isle. She was getting a tattoo and not batting
an eye. Don't let anyone deny that your mother was
something else. Later I heard you were born and that
she lived with your father in my ex's house.

Anyway, a very sixties entanglement. They're old

resentments, things you wouldn't understand; you don't have to inherit this karma. Forget the past, child, and live for the future, since you can.

One more thing: ask Yoko. She has a beauty salon in Miami, and everyone goes there. Not your mother—she didn't go to stylists. A kiss.

J. Pérez

P.S. Oh, and how did you find me, little girl? I'm in Canada, chopping down trees.

Nadia:

This is the idea I have of your mother, because it's been a very, very long time since I've heard from her: does she exist, or is she a figment of my imagination? I'm still in Havana, like always. The last time I saw her, I wrote this poem. I don't know if you'll find her in it, but maybe you'll recognize her.

A Many Splendored Thing

That you've been or are love
Two or three people's great love
They've told you many times
Dark enough times
Those two or three people.

In a moment they excuse themselves and check the hour
Or ask you what time it is

And it's almost always late, they're waiting, or not,
It doesn't matter.

They say goodbye staring at your eyes
Calmly pushing their hair back
As their great love closes the door
When they leave, feeling a bit guilty.

And once down the stairs
She asks what to do with two or three
Great treasures, what to do right now.

Ariel

Nadia:

Your mom came to Miami for a visit and stayed with
you-know-who. She never called me, didn't leave a
message. I'm still poor, but she's not.

It's a shame she abandoned you in Havana; she was
always more of a woman than a mother. Anyway, you
should look for her in galleries; I heard she caused
quite a stir and sold everything she'd brought. I never
understand anything. First, she was on the radio, and
now she sells art. Whatever—to each her own. We're all
crazy: look at Ana M., how she killed herself. Nobody's
happy with what they have, not even when they live in a
skyscraper.

I send you a kiss. Say hello to whatever's left of your
father, who must be in therapy if they're giving him so
many tributes over there.

Lula

Pretty girl:

I saw the catalogue for your *Luxury and Poverty* when it was in New York, but I found out about it too late and the show had already come down. It's a shame. I'm a soldier and don't want anything to do with those on the island, but you can't be blamed for any of that. I'd be happy to go see your work.

In 1979, I took photos of your and your mother's feet. That was around the time we went with her to Cienfuegos because Havana was . . . insufferable. I sold that diptych to some Hungarians so I lost sight of your feet. I hope they're still beautiful.

Your mother's around during art fairs. She's hanging out with a very dangerous person (I won't mention his name). I don't have her coordinates, but look for her in the Russian art world.

Kiss.

I hope you'll realize who this is.

Your admirer

Nadia:

I was a friend of your mother's.

I can tell you a bit more. I'll wait for you Friday at La Closerie des Lilas, 171 Boulevard du Montparnasse, Paris.

I have no flexibility on the date because I'm living in Milan and have very little free time. Friday, 9 p.m., dinner. I'm short and always wear a black suit and red tie.

Third table on the crystal terrace, on the left, that's my spot. Please confirm.

Paolo B.

CUBAN RADIO SOAP:
"MEETING PAOLO B."

SOUNDTRACK: *Italian music plays: Scarlatti, Sonata K 430. It's raining hard. A taxi stops at the entrance to the restaurant. A door opens and closes. A few brief words in French are exchanged.*

NARRATOR: *Carrying her disposable Chinese umbrella, Nadia gets out of the taxi and runs toward La Closerie des Lilas. The impeccable host at the door guides her to Paolo, who, diligent and chivalrous, helps her with her chair, first taking her red felt coat. Paolo looks her up and down and makes a strange face.*

SOUNDTRACK: *Italian music crossfades into cups, silverware, the ambience of a fine French restaurant.*

PAOLO B.: Nadia . . . your mother and I tried to make a life together, but she tends to start things and then destroy them. She could be the most brilliant and sensual spouse in the world. Then, the next month, she's bored, feels tied down, enclosed, has an existential breakdown, and flees. I was one of that lethal woman's victims.
No one can tie her down.

NADIA: Did you ever see her again?

PAOLO B.: About five years ago, at the door of the Chanel boutique, loaded down with packages. You go to Chanel for something, but it's vulgar to go to Chanel for everything. She was a luminous redhead then, talking in a clumsy Russian, with two children at her side and also a Russian gallery owner well-known and kind of a mafioso, who kept pawing and rearranging things nonstop. I wanted to kiss her hello, but she simply extended her hand demurely. I told her she looked beautiful, and she laughed one of her laughs, like yours, wrinkling her nose and raising her eyebrows as she lowered her chin. Your mother is the woman with the shortest memory in the world. Today she might recite your work, but tomorrow she expels you from her mind without asking permission.

She could be my wife, some Russian's wife, a great artist, a muse in Havana in the sixties; the hippie she's always been must be hidden somewhere. She's a lot of different women at once. It's going to be tough for you to find her. Your mom, I mean.

NARRATOR: *Paolo pours the wine and organizes the silverware for the second course. They finish their oysters and are now waiting for a steak tartare he ordered without consulting her.*

NADIA: Sorry, I know less about how to place the silverware than about my mother.

NARRATOR: *They smile and toast, having fun.*

PAOLO B.: It's impossible to know her. Her, I mean. At least I don't know anyone who's ever defined her in a way that made sense. She's blond sometimes, brunette sometimes, other times a redhead . . . I couldn't tell you who she is.

NADIA: I feel like I should go somewhere to . . . save her? I don't even know if that's the right word. I don't want to sound ridiculous, Paolo.

NARRATOR: *She tries to taste what's left in her cup, and Paolo, quickly and elegantly, takes it from her.*

PAOLO B.: Wait until they give you a new cup. I don't know if you like raw foods, but try the tartare, and we'll have some wine that used to make your mother more charming.

NADIA: I try to taste new things, to expand my palate. I want to get to know the world through my senses. My mother drinks wine?

PAOLO B.: Your mother drinks exotic wines, absinthe, and rum. She drinks life, your mom.

NADIA: Absinthe and rum? The best part is that if you drink absinthe ritually, it's like burning sugar; and rum is sugar. Are you Cuban? I don't think so.

PAOLO B.: Are you asking because of my accent? I didn't want to continue to be Cuban; it was a goal of mine. Nostalgia would wreck my plans; in fact, it's something that comes back, cyclically, and upsets my world. I've become someone from Milan. Otherwise I wouldn't have any of this. I live there, in an attic, and not in Havana. But in six hours I'll be in Guarda, lakeside, working. I used to be Cuban, but I'm not anymore.

NADIA: I didn't recognize your Cuban accent. You talk like a . . . Well, that's fine, I get it.

PAOLO B.: I asked you to meet me here to talk about your

mother. Since I can't tell you much more, it's probably best if you have your dessert with a friend who's also here, alone, sitting at that little table with the yellow light. He's a Russian artist. He has things to tell you about her. If you'll allow me, I'll get up, introduce you, he'll sit here, and I'll leave.

NADIA: That sounds like something out of a spy novel. I feel like a character out of *Seventeen Moments of Spring*. I don't understand why my mother would let go of someone as special as you.

PAOLO B., *smiling*: Don't flirt with me, don't wrinkle your nose, don't hide, because you're not making it easy . . . Can I ask you something before I leave?

NADIA: If it's about paying the bill, I'll try.

PAOLO B.: No, I pay the bills here at the end of the month. There are a lot of them and they pile up. This is like my house.

NADIA: I read on the internet that Anaïs Nin and Henry Miller used to come here with—

PAOLO B.: I want to ask you to accept this, but not for meals or books or materials. I want you to use the list of stores in this guidebook and this card in your name. I don't like seeing you in jeans; they're too vulgar for someone who reads Anaïs Nin and chooses that coat.

NARRATOR: *Nadia looks over the list and the platinum card. She stares at it and, practically holding her breath, puts it all back on the table.*

NADIA: This is too much for a poor artist like me. I don't know how to accept these sorts of gifts. This, in exchange for what?

PAOLO B.: "We're too poor to buy cheap." Give me one of your pieces. Something that's not as ephemeral as your mother. I want to make something clear before I leave. She never said she had a daughter, but you look too much alike. I believe you because you also come very highly recommended by the friends I have left in Havana.

NARRATOR: *Paolo B. hugs Nadia, gestures toward the Russian artist, who gets up and comes over to greet Nadia. The two men kiss goodbye, Russian style. Paolo leaves after they settle in. The Russian and Nadia make a Champagne toast.*

SOUNDTRACK: *Music rises . . . Rimsky-Korsakov. Scheherazade. The music then fades out with the final shot of the scene.*

MARCH 20, 2006, MOSCOW, RUSSIA, FORMER USSR

My mother has turned up. I take a cab to go meet her. Her old friends—former pariahs, guerrillas, hippie artists, poor people—are now executives, impresarios, successful people. The others got left behind along the way. They're either dead or no longer visible. The wall was taken down by the strong; the weak got buried under it.

My mother is here, in Moscow, with her adoptive children and her Russian husband. At the restaurant in Paris, the artist told me about my mother's photography. I went on the internet and found her gallery and, through that, figured out where she was in Moscow. I called, using the little Russian I had learned in school in Cuba, and managed to find her.

Moscow's streets are harsh and broad. Stern, perfectly drawn. It's awfully cold. A strong odor, like vinegar, creeps along them. It's a combination of fish, fruit, chocolate, and watered-down perfume. I feel my face hurt when the wind touches it. I haven't thought about visiting museums. Is Lenin's mummy still on display? I want to cross the bridge and go up the stairs to number 235 to meet my mother.

A letter from Saúl.

> *Nadia:*
> I have other things to do besides respond to your persecutions.
>
> I don't understand Cubans and their imbroglios. I went on vacation because I couldn't take it anymore. I'm busy with the small street groups we've been organizing in Buenos Aires for more than a year now. Do you remember my black notebook? I don't have time to waste.
>
> You've lied much more than me. Is your father dead or alive? He's being given a posthumous tribute organized by the Paris cinémathèque this summer. We have to see who's tracking who in this hunting game.
>
> Ana, in Buenos Aires, sends you a kiss. She says you know each other. Even if you don't want it, I'm including it with this letter. See you later. Merci.

As always, Saúl doesn't sign his letters.

Moscow is impotent. This is because of the cold.

My new Hogan boots are going to crack. Someone gives me a taste of nalivka (a very sweet liqueur). I write sheltered in an elegant café. I open a map to try to get oriented and read the guidebooks that make this endless territory so inviting.

I have to go to the Pushkin Museum, and I can't miss Red

Square, the Bolshoi. People seem very closed off here. I don't know this culture; we coexisted "long ago and far away," but the truth is the Soviets barely left a mark and we don't know much about them. Along the way, I've seen all kinds of boutiques and restaurants. This city is huge; the scale and the real-life dimensions are impressive. It has more than 10 million residents; the subway has 150 stops. I hate the concept of a subway.

RESTAURANT GUIDE

THE FIRST recommendation is the famous Café Pushkin, in a beautiful three-story building in Tverskaya, a fantastic and luxurious nineteenth-century mansion. It's the most glamorous place in the city for the rich, and surely jammed with tourists. The kitchen is open twenty-four hours, and the prices climb as you go up the stairs. The first floor is called Pharmacy, and dinner can be about sixty euros, but on the second and third floors you can spend as much as two hundred. It has nineteenth-century food, old-style cuisine, special recipes like, for example, some very light piroshki with several sauces, blini with caviar, game, and smoked fish. It all sounds very good, but I swear I have no idea what any of it tastes like; I think the Russians who lived in Cuba were maybe a little more modest in terms of their cooking. I remember sour cabbage-filled pastries and stuffed eggs. I remember going with my father to the Moscow restaurant in Havana, a place with varnished wood. My mother used to call it "the luxury stable." She left, but she left us her nicknames for things, her prejudices, her craziness rolling around in our heads. Sometimes I think when people die or disappear when they're young they can easily become myths: If they vanish quickly, they have that advantage. We don't get enough time to see them fall apart, have regrets, or disappoint us.

My father quotes her constantly; she's a classic, and it's his favorite thing to do. He feeds that ghost every day.

I'd love to ask my mother to that restaurant, maybe to the first floor dining room, the Pharmacy. But it'd be in bad taste to bring her to the place where the new Russian royalty drops its money. Now I'm on Krasnoznamennaya Street, just in front of the Hotel Mezhdunarodnaya. The owner of these businesses is the son of a popular actor: Oleg Tabakov. Well, I'm not hungry anymore. I came for my mother. Eating is secondary.

I almost didn't get the visa to come here. It seemed unbelievable, given how many Russians lived in Cuba, how much Russian food we ate, how much Russian fat (it was said to be seal fat), applesauce, preserves, Russian-Argentine meat. We even heard our lives in Russian. It's inconceivable they wouldn't let me in now.

I had a love-hate relationship with Russian cartoons. They could have been Russian, German, Polish . . . but we called them all Russian cartoons. We were solitary children, our parents always busy, the TV on, the screen in black and white bearing Russian letters.

My generation is marked by that. A Caribbean country raised with Soviet codes. I live in a cartoon: Mamushka lost and my father in a dacha far from Nadeshda, and me, a matryoshka rolling along in the real world. All my problems are stacked in order of size. They hide inside me. It can't be normal that I miss this: дядя стпа-милиционер (*Uncle Styopa,* a cop), *Mikrobi*, *The Princess Frog*, *The Electronic*, *Choky*, *Little Feather*, *The Grandchildren of the Cedar*, *The Abstaining Swallow*, *Little Bird Tari*, *The Adventures of Aladár Mézga*, *Thunder and Lightning*, *The Adventures of Anita*, *The Fröhliche Family*, *Apollonia Doll*, *Pavel* or *Palle Alone in the World*, *The Little Sandman*, and *Sour Milk*, with Fogón the mail carrier who brought us *Muñecos* magazine.

I'm a tourist in a country that, in some ways, I'm already familiar with. They made a great public intervention in Cuba. They left traces in our memories. We barely learned their language, and now they've forgotten us. Luckily, in a rapture about "indestructible friendships," I was able to snatch my visa and come looking for my mother.

Koniec.

I'm still in Moscow when I should have been in New York. That's the story. I've interviewed all of my mother's friends who responded to my call. How can people describe the same person with so much contradiction? She has a thousand faces. I've brought my father's films. One of them has her name as its title.

I've called Cuba without luck. Where's my father now?

The cab driver says we're here. I say, *Spasiva*. He responds, *Merci*.

I knocked on the door. They didn't expect me. They talked to me in Russian, then in French. They asked what I wanted.

They wouldn't let me in until I could explain myself. As I did, I surveyed what was inside from the door. I was finally allowed in. I took my shoes off and stepped on the Persian rug. My naked feet followed the velvet route to my mother. They weren't drinking tea from a samovar. They were watching TV and eating burgers, drinking Coke. My mother was sitting on the sofa, sipping her tea; she was the only face familiar to me in the living room. She offered me her cup. She wasn't that different from other Cuban women. She looked so much like me! My emotion increased with the mystery. What an ache!

I remembered her young and beautiful in that hyperrealist painting at Havana's Museum of Fine Arts in which she appeared to be lying on the grass. The years have changed her completely; the painting remains the same. Were her black eyes asking me who I was and what I wanted from her? I didn't feel love. I thought we were recovering a moment, assured by being together in a secret place.

Today is March 20th. Are they celebrating something? What are they celebrating? It doesn't matter. As my father says: "I'm here because I've arrived."

I kissed my mother with an ordinary gesture and realized her perfume was the same as mine, Rive Gauche, and considered it a trap my father had set. I sat on the sofa. Little by little, I transformed into someone who lets herself attempt the impossible. I grabbed the remote and turned down the volume, changed the channels. I couldn't understand the newscast. I just really wanted to start somewhere, to vary the images, but everything can't be changed in a day.

My mother looked at me strangely, like a bird lost inside a supermarket. I had stretched out in front of her and was on the verge of sleep. The oldest daughter had arrived. The prodigal daughter was in Moscow, at home, in any one of my mother's houses. A little more and I might have reached nirvana, but then I remembered: Where's my father now?

"*Merci*," I said as I sipped my mother's tea.

Someone came with a blanket and tucked us in. I closed my eyes again . . . and that was it. I don't remember anything else.

Good night, Dear Diary. *Merci*, Moscow.

I've arrived in Paris, with Moscow behind me and my mother waiting: plane, train, car, Saché-Calder.

I check my email. I call Havana, but there's no answer.

Letter from Diego:

Hi Nadia,
First, I want to thank you for letting me see the sculptures at the Calder before anyone else. Being alone in that castle was amazing.

I think you forgot about my trip, but luckily I was able to get the keys and now here I am, snooping through your things, checking them out. I'm looking at your heroes as they freeze, burn, and melt; they freeze, burn, and melt forever, even before you can get over them.

To see them disappear at night and reappear in the morning is magic.

Your assistants work quickly. I imagine you as some kind of tyrant giving orders. A little socialist tyrant, to be exact: a new kind of tyrant. The truth is, I can't imagine you giving orders at all.

To be here with the sculptures, before them, a minute before the world sees them: it's a real privilege and, even more, a pleasure.

You're the woman who's brought me the most pleasure. To touch, to look, to feel, to smell, to think. Even losing you has been a pleasure.

I loved your previous show, *Luxury and Poverty*, so much! But this is greater; it reaches much greater heights. You start to look up, and suddenly it just flattens you with its spiral. Between the faces, the uniforms, and the constant return to the country of our memories, your mother—or mine—appears, your father—or mine—and I don't know, you can't stop. Your head's disorganized, but your subconscious, yes. It's as if all that's lyrical and epic about that entire nation, a place that belongs to me because I love it like I love you, was brought together in those articles of clothing.

It's so good to be without you and at your side; I swear it feels like when I land in Havana.

You weren't here . . . Is this one of your jokes? You wanted our encounter to be with your work and not with the naughty devil you are and have always been to me? I don't know.

In any case, I'm going back to Mexico soon, without seeing you, all the way from the frozen Paris of my adolescence, from the fiery Havana of our childhood. Between heroes and tombs, I remember you . . . Nadia. We're on the verge of the World Cup. You can imagine what that means for a journalist like me. I'm at attention: at war, mobilized. But I'm leaving "happy and nude," as someone I never forget once said.

Kisses, and thank you for the empty bed, which is
huge. Thank you for the "tea and sympathy" of your
absence. I like it more with each passing day.

Yours,
Diego

P.S. My father doesn't remember when he last saw your
mother. I'm sorry. I think it's best he forget.

Uff! Good God! I forgot Diego would be in Paris. He wrote
me. I was half asleep, but I sent him the coordinates so he
could spend a few days with me. It can't be. My mother! My
life! My head can't deal with all this. I'm down. I try to remember the song Diego liked when we were nine years old.
Wait . . . I have it right here.

I go to my laptop to add it to my infinite radio playlist. I send
it to him as a gift. A part of the program for Diego. A piece of
audio art. A fragment to offer relief for my carelessness. Radio
helps solitary people, insomniacs. In their lethargy, they hear
a voice, an accent, or a melody, and that awakens certain feelings. The furious business that has our heads going in circles,
going night and day, resists the dream.

A PROGRAM FOR DIEGO

Good night, Diego. This program is for you. Just you. I finally found my mom. I had to flee before you got here. I couldn't wait for anything. I couldn't think. I left as soon as I could. I took my coats and the map of her face in my daze. Before I go on, I'm going to give you a song. When we were nine years old, we used to sing it together in the sound booth where we made the show *Good Morning, Little Friends*. Everyone used to laugh at how you tried to hide your Mexican accent when you talked on official channels. Do you remember this song? "Ugly (*Lo feo*)" by Teresita Fernández.

> *The things that are ugly*
> *give them a little love . . .*

My Diego: When I was in Moscow, I didn't see anything that moved me in any special way; it was as if I'd seen it all before. The only thing that shook me was my mother's face aghast. I swear, dear Diego, that finding her has meant losing myself. I have to go back home, but holding her hand. I should guide her. She's left her body. She's incoherent, delirious. Her mind is hidden in darkness, submerged, and I can't find it. It's curious because sometimes she nails it in spite of the nonsense, but I know she's not the same woman we lost sight of when we were ten.

Do you remember her directing our children's programs from behind the console, talking nonstop from her mic into our headphones?

She's not the same. We went to the Pushkin Museum together, but she didn't pay attention to the work so I was unfocused throughout the first exhibition. I didn't take notes in my diary. She seemed nervous, trying to get out of there, her eyes betraying how far away she was.

The line to get in was interminable. Later I understood it was really two lines, and the longer one took us to an exhibition about Coco Chanel. It was very instructive; Mami only dresses in Chanel now. I want to repatriate her, take her back to Cuba for reasons you'll understand, but I can't imagine her dressed like that on the streets of Havana.

We went into the museum and it was spectacular: Goyas, Matisses, Monets, Toulouse-Lautrecs. I wanted to take my time looking at them, but I was anxious, still guiding my mother; I didn't want to lose her in the crowd.

Well, Diego, I'll tell you what was going on while you were waiting for me at the Calder and I was finding my mother in Moscow.

This time, on this program just for you: the Moscow subway.

Did you know the stations are decorated in a very special way? Each is different: columns, gigantic recessed lights, high-hanging lamps, sculptures that allude to the new Soviet man. Without a doubt, it's an homage to the countryside, to the worker, to the athlete, to Lenin, Lenin, Lenin.

The Bolshoi and its surroundings were undergoing a remodel. Even so, I was able to see *The Queen of Spades*, based on Pushkin's story with music by Tchaikovsky. They say the theater is built over the river so the acoustics will be impeccable. This whole area is full of very pleasant restaurants.

Finally, the most essential part of all this, where we always wanted to go when we were kids. Do you remember?

My dear and only listener tonight. You probably know Red Square is a rectangle, and the horizontal sides are so very long. On one side, the Kremlin with its many buildings, palaces, and churches, topped by the mausoleum that houses a mummified Lenin. On the other side, a commercial center, an authentic temple to capitalism. The many boutiques are expensive and exclusive, so Comrade Lenin must be spinning in his grave.

Sunday in Red Square: the line to get into the mausoleum is endless, but I had to see it. Otherwise, how to get rid of this macabre Cuban curiosity I've had all my life? The necrophilia inspired by that photo of the dead Che began to creep up inside me. In the end, Lenin was lying in there and I was out here, not able to see him. No, no, and no.

Let's listen to a song together, my dear Diego, and I'll go on with my story. A kiss at midnight, from the modulated frequency of my little sound machine.

Do you remember in Havana, how we'd climb under the blankets in our little tent with just our flashlight? I wonder if we were born to live in tents. Listen to this hymn. I bet you haven't forgotten the words . . .

I'm a Pioneer with my whole heart
And I'll camp eagerly.
I'll make knots and camp . . .

That explorer's song brings back so many memories, Diego. I can't imagine you driving around Mexico City and singing this song from our childhood. Never mind narrating a soccer game during the World Cup and suddenly hearing you say: "A blue sky and an arena like a child's drawing." We're bipolar. How long will we have to resist these memories? Can we possibly block out all we were?

Let's continue with Lenin.

The hardship passed quickly. Two hours with nothing to read while standing in line under the open sky. I'd brought only Derrida with me, and I didn't want to weigh down Red Square. Even though I was trained for this sort of thing, I was a nervous wreck. I looked around, checked out every corner of the square. I opened a notebook and drew six sketches from different angles. Finally, just as I was about to become one of my ice sculptures, Lenin.

They practically undressed me at the door, and they made me pay to leave my coat. I was left in my underwear: a sleeping shirt and long ballet leggings. That was the worst: to stand there in my undies under the somber mausoleum light. And to think I don't take off my coat even to go to the bathroom. I'm not familiar with the culture of dressing for the cold. This was me, Nadia, a replicant for Lenin's widow, in my underwear, flying like a butterfly around the specter. They took my cell phone; they even took my modesty. This all happened in a very bad way. There was incomprehensible yelling in English and mobilizing and dramatic Russian shrieks. But, my dear, I'm used to that.

Oh, Diego: how amazing it is to complain on your own private independent radio show about the things you can't complain about on the air! This is such a relief!

Diego, dear, I haven't asked you if you've ever been there. The ritual: the entry, you go around the yellow mummy, you can't pause, never mind trying to look for any sustained period of time. And then it seemed like Vladimir was going to wink at me and say: "Nadeshda, my wife, get me out of here—I've been on view far too long!" but I was shoved out of there instead.

My whole life dreaming of that specter. It was just exactly as we imagined it as kids.

I was always frightened by Lenin's face. He'd appear to me in my nightmares. I loved the shivers I got when I was scared. Now I just feel terror. It's not the same to imagine him as it is to see him lying there for eternity.

At the end of my trip, when we were saying goodbye, I talked to my mother's husband. She's suffering from a serious breakdown of her central nervous system. It could be Alzheimer's, but they're not sure. The Russian wants to get rid of the problem. He would give her back to me with her papers and everything.

Diego, do you think I should take her back to Cuba? Her adoptive children aren't having luck communicating with her. She's a burden on everyone. They would abandon her like she once abandoned us. Everything comes back to the same point. I compare today with yesterday, and I don't understand her. If she was leaving something so terrible behind, why did she leave me behind in the terribleness?

She has to be taken care of. She's very thin and cries all the time. She speaks gibberish and only in Spanish. She doesn't recognize me. I'm rootless. Without a past. Homeless. I feel like someone's pulling me back, grabbing me by the back of my coat as I try to step forward.

Tell me if you've been to Russia.

Tell me what you remember of me. How was I the first time we met? I've lost track of that day. I don't know where I'm from.

I want to adopt my mother. I'm going to close my own circle.

Listen . . . Don't forget this broadcast is just for you. Here's a song your father used to love. Vicente Feliú sings it. Remember?

Believe me
when I tell you I'm going with the wind . . .

Goodbye, Diego. Sorry about my hyperrealist song; I hope you remember it and get a good sleep after listening to this. A kiss on the cheek until we see each other again, here or walking on this earth.

Remember that you've just spent . . . *Daybreak with No One.*

LETTER FROM DIEGO, ATTACHED TO MY RED DIARY

Nadia, little girl . . . :
What a lovely program you sent me. I'm so lonesome, I don't know how to thank you. Of course, the memories from working at the radio station come back to me. Cuba is marvelous—its music and light are enough to make you forget the bad moments. I admire your strength and support, what you're doing for your mother; it makes me wonder if I couldn't be doing more for my father. I now realize we're a totally screwed up generation, like our parents' memories.

I have a lot to tell you about you, but I'd rather do it in person. I never lose that hope, even though you always stand me up.

I've lost sight of the first image of you. I remember your mother's shapely legs. Her hand dragging you along; you wore black. I've never again seen a nine-year-old girl wearing black, as if in mourning. Only someone like her could have designed such a dress for a girl with such sparkling eyes. Of course, we were dealing with scarcities and emergencies, but it was odd to see that color on your body at such a young age.

I close my eyes.

I see you eating toasted meal with sweetened condensed milk while watching TV at my house. You told me that day you didn't have one at your house.

You marched with me in a marching band next to a row of boys. You were the "minor baton," marching up front, your hair short, moving your little Cuban butt to the beat. You held my hand whenever it wasn't at your waist. You were serious when you marched, looking straight ahead, toward the parade's finish line.

I'll never forget when you learned the Mexican national anthem for my birthday, but you got the words mixed up and said some pretty weird things. I don't know where you got that version.

The day they handed out toys: Basic/Not Basic/ Directed.

Your mother didn't get to the store on time and they wouldn't let my father go in with you. You lost your turn. I remember your face when you saw me come out of the store with my lavish box of toys. You had nothing and looked desperate. Later, we played ball and soccer. Me with my toys, you with nothing. I still feel guilty: they were toys for Cuban kids and I was a foreigner. You showed me how to bat. You played like a macho tomboy on the field.

I never understood two things: Why are you so feminine, so flirty, so beautiful, and, at the same time, so firm and resolute?

Where were your parents?

You're the only Cuban girl who bathed in the sea practically in the nude. I loved seeing you wear just the bottoms of your bikini.

The day I left, you said, "I'm always going to be your girlfriend, maybe even the mother of your children."

You were laughing as you kissed my mouth, and then you left, walking slowly toward your father's house, just across the street from ours. You didn't say goodbye. Your mother was already wandering the earth, and your father was just a shadow who tried to take care of you.

Later, we saw each other, but we weren't kids anymore. That was my big moment with you.

Yes, I've been to Russia. I didn't want to see Lenin. I don't like going back to the past. Only your body makes me go back.

I've never forgotten the subject: "mother."

Today is too much for me.

I'll call you tomorrow; I'd rather hear your voice. Listen, Cuban girl, turn on your cell, please. You know: I adore you.

Diego

I'm not going to answer your calls, Diego.

My family is vanishing and you're all that's left. My mother's like a game of jacks, her memory in pieces, untethered from her broken intelligence.

Papi gets programmed even in retrospectives of dead Latin American film directors.

My father is who agonizes me.

I walk among the dead, continue working on my projects as if I were wearing army boots, using what little courage I have left to do them.

You're the only sure thing in my life. I'd run to you and ask you to marry me. Once convinced, we'd live happily and in peace. But there's one thing I know for sure: I can't be happy until I close this circle, until I deal with the death of my parents.

I can't answer your calls. Or see you. If I did, I'd leave everything to be a normal woman. I've always had the opportunity to leave my traumas if I were by your side. Living with you means not having an excuse to complain or disobey. And it's not the right time.

Nadia

P.S. Today is April 4, Day of the Pioneers.

LETTER FROM DIEGO IN MY RED DIARY

APRIL 6, MEXICO CITY

Nadia:
Enough already of trying to idealize your projects and
your existence: your essential aspiration is harmony.
We Jews always sing what we've never had: shalom,
peace. In a Catholic scheme, where what's relevant isn't
life on earth but what comes after, very little matters.
In Buddhist thinking, we simply complete the circle of
one of many lives, and there's no problem either. The
truth is, working within these concepts, we don't live; we
simply yearn for those who come after us to live more
comfortably.

Please, my dear girl—sister—woman—mythical creature,
be happy however you want, just be happy.

When we met, you, my father, and I were in Cuba
because of something having to do with Trotsky's death.
Worse, actually: Trotsky's murder. I've never wanted to
know what it was, and I don't want to know now, but my
father has never found peace, and I don't want to share
in his schizophrenia.

Nadia: I don't understand why you insist on suffering.
It breaks you apart and destroys you. Aren't you still the
heroine I once knew?

The wars you sign up for aren't yours—they're not yours or our parents' either. You have to choose your battles, even when other forces insist that, in fact, the crusade of the day involves us and that we should be grateful for the gallons of blood shed.

You have to choose your enemies and their battles. Be a little more afraid of your head than of your surname.

Little Nadia, thank you again for your radio show. I listen to it every night as I go to sleep. You guessed what can keep me awake. You're my lullaby. I have serious problems falling asleep; at these hours of the night, I'm also visited by old ghosts I've inherited. It kills me to confess I've been cowardly. I don't think it makes sense to lie about something like that.

Would you believe this confession? I've never again said "I love you." Just to you, just in Havana, just to you.

Yes, when I've gone back to your island, I've seen it: half of Cuba has changed. What's left? The dream of the past?

Your mother used to say something my father still repeats: "The dog has four legs but chooses only one path."

Whenever you want to come down that road, let me know.

Always yours,
Diego

DEAR DIARY

LIST OF MY MOTHER'S LOVERS

Coco	Armando
Pablo	Nicolás
Sebastián	Waldo
Lujo Rojas	Paolo B.
Enrique Díaz Caballero	Ed
Jorge Maletín	Gabriel
The troubadour	Ernesto
The scissors sharpener	Lama

It's April 12 and Paris is killing me. I have to run through this list of names. The idea is to conquer those people who can tell me about my mother. She doesn't say much.

I'm going to see Paolo B. tonight. I pick out some new lingerie in a very interesting store. Every one needs to be conquered in their own way. I don't plan on giving up.

I'll do whatever I need to do to find out how my mother used to be. I have no scruples now; I left them all behind in Havana.

I make choices as I go through what's on the hangers. Black lingerie strikes me as ridiculous. Better I get the red. I love lingerie—I love the designs. They speak of the body; they express themselves in a fantastic dialogue between nudity and transparency. I buy two skimpy pieces to scare Paolo B.

There's a doorman at Paolo's building who calls ahead so Paolo knew I was there before I went up. He opens the door wearing a silk Japanese robe and so much cologne it could flood the city.

The walls are full of enormous paintings, mostly by Cuban artists. It's impressive to see a giant Servando in Paris. An Amelia Peláez under halogen lights. The Portocarrero vibrates on the wall, makes a sound like music. A tiny sketch of a bull by Picasso. There's a seascape by Romañach, a piece of Varadero hanging in the corner, as moist as if it'd just stopped raining. Graffiti on a piece of glass:

"Are you always attracted to damaged women?"
"I didn't know there were any other kind."
—*Philip Roth*

Paolo B. brought me a glass of a wine my mother used to like.
No music.
The soft sound of the humidifier and whatever was cooking in the kitchen.
"Are you on your way back? How is she?"

"I've come for a list."

"A list of people who might be able to find her?"

"That one I have. Now I need to know who she is."

Paolo tried to take off my coat, but I didn't let him. I had a surprise for him. He looked at me like an old wolf who realizes he has prey on his hands. I played the naughty girl. It was a silent arrangement—whatever was going to happen would happen as soon as he took off my coat. I can't believe what I'm about to do, but I'm having a lot of fun.

"Let me try to help you with your list. Maybe I can round it out."

"What's for dinner?"

"A cultish meal from your generation, Cuban girl: Saint-Germain purée, cheese omelette, white rice, and a banana placed in the corner of the plate."

"Peas, omelette, rice, and plantains—just like during the best of times in the boarding schools out in the country."

"The staff just left, so if you want something else you'll have to make it yourself."

I took off my coat in one swift move and leapt over to Servando's painting—I didn't break anything in the process.

I remembered when I did gymnastics at school and my father demanded precision and concentration. The pirouettes were calculated; my Russian twirls always hit their mark. I was a champion, and no one could ever take that from me. I got even with my defeats by then winning medals.

I made several turns. I used to go to real extremes with my exercises. Pirouettes so precise I never knocked over a jar or broke any ornate object, like the ones making a rare appearance in Paolo's living room.

He thought I'd be nude, that that's why I wasn't taking off my coat. But I was better dressed than an army general in a parade.

Now I'm in the air, almost touching the halogen lights, in perfect balance with the night, on top of the radiators, like a circus monkey going for a triple into his arms.

I landed in one piece in his embrace and bit his lip instead of kissing him. Paolo won't give me any credit for that performance. We both knew it was all a trick: static and dynamic movements artificially programmed. An artistic gymnast. Nobody lies better than a Cuban in this situation. "Lie to me again," I thought I heard him say.

He'd realized I was completely dressed, uniformed; he'd registered my strong thighs; he'd caught sight of my well-trained, firm body with his angry eyes. I was a Pioneer with my bandana and everything. A communist Pioneer snuck into his house! What is this? I was suddenly on his mouth, kissing him coldly and awkwardly, the way experts like him like. Really awkwardly so he could teach me later. They want to teach us, and we need to let ourselves be taught. I learn everything to the last detail; my list is full of dictators. I like dictators in bed. Why deny that in this very senseless situation?

We made love standing up, against the glass with the graffiti. The Pioneer remained dressed after all. Paolo is an expert when it comes to separating interiors; he nearly suffocated me with my bandana as he penetrated me over and over, and over again. I kicked the lamp in the corner and didn't care if it was a Tiffany—it didn't matter; whatever I broke was much less than what I was doing to my mother.

Paolo carried me to the sofa. He tore my uniform to pieces; my heart was beating wildly. And even in the moment, I thought the act of ripping was terrible, especially my Pioneer uniform. I hit him hard and climbed up, as if I were grabbing the balance beam, using him as a longitudinal axis. I've always longed to be an athlete when it came to love, my mind blank, my body ready. His slap came fast. A quick twist of the hand destroyed my skirt, and it was such a beautiful and cruel act.

What would we say the next day at school? I was terrified and anxious. Myth destroyed.

I love taming the old wolf. Leaping about together, as if we were fleeing. Traveling far, to an intermediate place—not Cuba, not France, not him, not Mami, not me. A place like us. My sex swallows him as if he were a Chinese plum, and I feel Paolo so wet that he traverses me and arrives at a place completely unknown. Although he may want to deny his instinct, his body is his country.

I cast aside all the women I've been with other men. His sex hurts me, and I tremble as he splits me in two. He's already won.

May he remember nothing, may he dismiss his guilt and fears. May he destroy what he needs; I'm the force that awaits him, and I win by being destroyed. Balanced and centered. The hidden diameter between my legs. Paolo is below me. I slip and fall dead. I can't contain my groan. I'm down on the mat.

My childish laughter ruins everything. Paolo is the most intense man I've ever met. His anger has turned to candor; maybe the waters from my body blessed the most amnesiac Cuban in the world with a little tenderness.

I was dying of desire and he was dying of happiness. It's quite the trip to Cuba he's taking with me on this sofa. We bruised each other and caressed each other. Wounds and caresses. Kisses and ardor. Hard, soft, slow, sweet. An adagio, a kind of pain that transformed into pleasure until we both shattered. I felt Paolo inside me like no one else. I decided to nap as he served the meal, the same menu as our country school. It was more like a meal from the Champs-Élysées.

I didn't let him see me in the nude. I told him it was a tradition from school. We had to get our uniforms signed before we graduated. I showed him my back and asked him to jot down the names of my mother's other lovers on my white shirt.

Paolo tore the shirt off me.

"In my generation, we got tattoos. We were a little braver than yours. Your mother had a compass rose on her back. Do you want the names or not?" he said, almost threateningly. He had a little gadget in his hand to emboss and color. I could tell from his fingers he wanted to start everything again.

I turned back to my own desire, moist on the sofa. I don't know how we'd gotten the upholstery so wet. Paolo may be less to my mother, but to me he's already too much. Sex must have been very hard in the '60s. Is that why I was born? Anyway . . . I waited until he went to the kitchen and put on my coat. I wrote with my lipstick on the same graffitied glass: "The last Pioneer was here."

I pulled the door open. I left without the list. I didn't say goodbye.

Dear Diary: I'm going back to Cuba.

Part II

PAIN AND FORGIVENESS

The girl you still are would like to take shelter,
but there is none . . .
You walk barefoot, Laila, on the ruins of your homeland.

—JORGE VOLPI

CUBA STAYS IN CUBA

Since Cuba stays in Cuba and can't be transported anywhere else, I'm back here. I've come to bury my father. The graves and the flowers are here; the theaters with celebrity names and the jewels that got lost in the chaos. The beaches for swimming alone in the deep, blurry with whirling sand, blinding seaweed, and the dust from sifting shells.

I hear the laughter of those who swam with me in the first and second tiers of my childhood. They went on, but I've come back, I insist, to swim in the sea in my beach of memories. "We're poor," my mother would say when the afternoons ended on those beaches, and I'd be hungry as we waited for a truck to go home, or a lost bus that would stop for us at dusk. "We're very poor, Nadia."

I keep photos of the wreckage, the books upon books with and without homemade dust jackets read during the endless summer vacation of my life. I'm like an unhappy summer, like Saturday night parties covered in confetti, forgotten beers, and *trova* concerts on a stairway or black sand.

I am my last summer and the first of many without my father. One thing I know for sure: after experiencing snow, I'm not the same. I came fleeing the cold, and I'm welcomed by a frigid humidity.

The cold has stripped my skin of that perennial and liberating nakedness the heat had bequeathed to me. I've forgotten how to put up with the heat without complaint. Now the challenge is to bring the sun back to my skin, to forget the crushing presence of winter. Enough! The heat here doesn't let you think. But don't sweat it—the north sweeps away pieces of the Malecón, and that's all the cold we get. This is Havana. That's how it is. And how it challenges me!

I don't understand much through my Russian lens. This is Havana; you deal with it straight, no playing around.

From the airport to the hospital, all night waiting for my father's death, and then, at dawn, to the museum. I go back to the contemporary art room every time to pray for those who are no longer here.

This is Havana. Mudéjar, neoclassical, art nouveau—it resists but still reveals the remains of an architecture that can't be defined. This is Havana. For Uncle Matt, travelers mean ruin, the city conquered by Orientales—not the Chinese or Asian Indian kind but Orientales from the Eastern side of the island, cradle of the son. For others, the city is a sun-filled theater or a geriatric clinic. For me, it's a museum where I come to rescue what's left.

The hospital has smoked glass. Salt covers the views of the grayish sea. The salt advances! From here you can see the unforgiving sea taking back the pieces once stolen from it.

APRIL 18

AS IN any good drama my father has waited for me to return before he will die.

I cry to make him think I understand. But I don't understand; actually, this feels like a conspiracy against me—it can't be that I will have no one left who's lucid. The nurse hears me talking with a psychiatrist friend of my father's and interrupts us as she injects my father with morphine.

"Girl," she says, "forget about it. They're going to drive you crazy."

As the poet Reina María says: "They're going to drive me crazy, yes, just like everyone wanted."

How can they want me to forget? Could it be the entire country has agreed to forget? Maybe I wasn't tipped off and so I'm defenseless. They forget the sick a little before burying them. It's all about avoidance. They prep themselves for that nonchalance.

I go down to the hospital lobby. Lujo Rojas waits for the shift change at seven. (Lujo is my father's real widow.)

Now everything depends on the morphine, his kidneys, and the chess game my father wants to play. My father is bisexual and could seduce even death. He was always trying to cast a spell on anyone, at any time. Lujo was his lover before leaving in the '70s; my father and I still live in his house.

He came back two months ago for his mother's death, which turned into a melodrama; she was a famous television presenter. This country is a cemetery. Now my father's ex-lover is trying to find a way to stay in Cuba. He's come back and wants to resist; he has nowhere else to go in this world. "*Lujo*—'luxury.' 'Luxury is red' was his catchphrase." I've never understood the nuance.

Lujo inherited from his mother a large house by the sea;

it faces the Malecón. When you look at it you can't help but wonder: who lives there, putting up with all that salt? When my father dies, I'll remain with Lujo, resisting the salt. Lujo has been the most lucid of my parents. The third leg of the table. Outside Cuba, he couldn't get it together to figure out his old age, but here he even planned my birth. Unbelievable!

Now we'll come to an agreement. He's going to take in my mother for at least three months, then we'll see. The bureaucracy wears me down, and he's already got his way back figured out. We know my father won't die without saying what he wants to say to everyone. We have to wait until he's a little better, listen, and let him go. Lujo knows him so well!

This is Havana. This is Lujo. We're both back, finally. Things can start to change. Even if it's bad, at least it will be a change.

MY COUNTRY:
MY PERSONAL MUSEUM

My country has been posing for the world since long before I was born.

I take Lujo to the contemporary art room at the Museum of Fine Arts. (The '80s and '90s.) Lujo is a painter. He inaugurated pop art in Cuba and has been banned here more than Celia Cruz, but they still exhibit his work in the museum. Kept under lock and key, various painters: Lujo, Julio—my first love—my mother lying on the grass . . . everything that was alive for us is now museumable.

"How old are you now, Nadia? You look like an old woman when you get nostalgic, when you complain, when you talk . . . Everything that happened to me is happening to you, even with your sweet little girl face."

We journey through the past: people, places. Lujo wants to know if my parents have prepared me. He asks me about Martínez Pedro and territorial waters, about Tania Bruguera's *Statistic*, woven out of human hair, a promiscuous intervention we've all gone through while waving flags; the bathroom tiles Alejandro Aguilera remade while covering the word "Revolution" with shards from his own house and body; the bow of the working-class instrument René Francisco pulls from oil paints; Glexis Novoa's Russian and ensemble-iconic master plans; Elso's sacred hand; Bedia's isolated men; and the void in the white walls waiting for those yet to come, like a boomerang in the shape of an island.

In the midst of this "red fantasy," Lujo is delirious about being shown among the younger classics.

"Are you not museumable yet?" my old and new friend sneers.

"No, I'm ephemeral." Not even the MoMA can conserve me.

"Soon, soon. You'll see. Life is just a breath, my dear . . . and everything is catchable from the front, against a wall. That's when they'll begin to murder your style."

My bridge is between the '80s and '90s. It's those ramps that take me from one decade to the next. I try to catch and keep the things I love—that's why I like museums and not cemeteries. The art of stopping, conserving, grasping. That's also why I like Havana: this city is a museum not yet collapsed in the midst of a strange battle to protect its shine. My time is sepia; my pain, salty; my scent is the essential oil from that old, old perfume, those traces (or remains?) of Chanel in remote bottles, like my own memories of this indefinite age.

The curtains and the balconies, the sculptures and the buildings. Ideas and words, posters and vinyl records, bricks and lace. Palimpsest. Life under layers of paint, between hidden letters no one can silence.

Country, personal museum, rituals, echoes.

FUNERAL SPEECH.
HAVANA IN THE RAIN

THURSDAY, APRIL 20

We weren't in Paris during a downpour, but "downpour" was the best word to describe what was falling on my head. The sound hit my forehead, my body, my height, and it hurt. The man in charge of the green light to success at the national film institute, that melancholic and elusive man with a Belgian accent and dictatorial smile, said a few words about my father.

I don't understand why it wasn't one of his photographers, or Lujo, who spoke. I don't know. Anyway. Apparently I'm not made to understand but to feel anger, all the anger in the world during this funeral, which is in such bad taste.

Grandstand. Speakers. The circus of death. Again, the circus of death. I hate the collective meaning of death. But everything is collective here. I don't even know if sex here can still be a thing for two; in fact, I've made love many times between bunk beds full of people talking, singing, and hurrying us along as accompaniment. I open Lujo Rojas's gray umbrella. He won't stop crying, expressing a pain I didn't know existed.

He's someone else who likes to give to and receive pain from his neighbor. I can't tolerate that. I spot people who love or loved my father very much, and people who just love to be near the tragedy of others. I won't be able to review how I really feel until I get home. How stupid it was to hear the apology addressed to my dead father when we all know that, in life, he was sentenced to silence! But I didn't have the courage to tell them to shut up.

I cry because I never cry. My only reaction is to escape. I leave them, I'm leaving. I don't care if their eyes pierce my back. No one here can comfort me. I walk away to get closer to my father. I walk on the wet grass poking out from Colón Cemetery's white concrete and think about the times he filmed here. I sink into this tragedy of Lalique crystal and Carrara marble loved by the Cuban aristocracy.

This death means the end of what began with my paternal grandparents' patrimony, this endless socialism that separated them from my father. Now we can rest, leaning on the sad and expensive glass that decorates their graves. After rejecting what we would have inherited from them, we now accept this last feast and go headlong into the grave, where they'll bury us in their elegant pantheons.

Although life was humble and miserable, what little we have left is here, in opulent death. In the end we will find ourselves in the same magnificent place. Now I enter a ransacked crypt. Bones, glasses, snails, rosemary, weeds. I see what I see—what do you see?

An angel missing an arm.

A tiger missing a copper ball.

A girl with a broken tiara holding a glass of dead flowers.

A strange flower with its marble stem rebuilt with plaster.

There's a confusing text: "Arturo: We remind you of what you took without telling us." God!

I see what I see—what do you see?

I see Saúl running in the rain. Saúl running in the rain? He hugs me as if all this hurts. But what is Saúl doing here? He lives in Barcelona. This is a nightmare.

"Nadia, I'm getting wet. Can you share your umbrella?"

"What are you doing here?" I ask as I cover him.

"It was true, your father was alive. I never believed you. Your father was a great filmmaker. I've seen his work."

"But since when are you in Cuba? What is this?"

"I came to photograph the Plaza de la Revolución after the celebrations. A foundation has given me money to salvage the remains of flags and posters. Ah! Your father's documentary on Cuban political symbols is very good. What an amazing vision he had of the circus during the seventies!"

"Fuck you, Saúl. Do me a favor and get out from under my umbrella, because your opportunism is contagious. Get out from under my umbrella, or I'm going to bury you alive in the tomb of the counts of Pozos Dulces. Go, go, and have some respect: it may be a circus, yes, but it's my circus . . . Now you're here to drink from the water that seemed so cloudy to you. Get wet, asshole. Get wet because this is Cuba and it really rains here; it's not the light pitter-patter that will make you sick. A lightning bolt will kill you here. Get wet with what I grew up on; bathe in this downpour to see if you'll finally become a man. I hope you drown while shooting photos of flags. You're so cowardly! Get out of my sight, Saúl. You don't know me."

I turn my back on him and lose myself among the graves. This is pathetic. My father doesn't deserve this, but I've already allowed it. I can't go up against the institutions, the cynics, and the madness. You don't own your own pain here. What did I expect? I'm going home.

As the rain rages, the many actors in this play my father put together scatter. The wind stirs voices I hear in the distance: Sorry. Prohibited. Courage. Daring. Suffering. Revolution. Rehabilitation. Return. Return. Parameterization. Understanding. Reconsider. Every five minutes: "Sorry." That word is a slap in the face.

I move away from their false spirit of mourning. Running to the cemetery gate, the man from the institute who spoke passes by me and almost trips. He runs as if he's afraid of being trapped with the others. Everyone is dead except him.

This ending doesn't resolve what they've done to my parents. Nadia, Nadia, think a little. Couldn't it be your parents allowed themselves to have this done to them? This can't be an accident.

Saúl grabs a cab as he takes two or three photos—videos?—of this gated graveyard. First he rejects us because of the way we misuse our political circumstances; now he takes advantage of those circumstances. Not one more dead. I can't stand this wake, which now extends to my body.

APRIL 23

LUJO AND I are moving. Like two old women, we run around the old house, picking up photos, forgotten tapes, books with and without dust jackets. At last we can cry without witnesses.

"Nadia, your father didn't get a chance to say what he wanted. He didn't have time."

"If my father went like that, it was because that's all he had to say." I knew him very well.

"Don't be cruel."

"But I knew him."

"Me too."

"Where did you get to know him so well, huh?"

We laugh. We cry together and open a bottle of wine. He told me how he courted both my father and my mother because otherwise my mother wouldn't have allowed the relationship. God, what a weird couple! What a weird trio! Actually, my parents' marriage was an agreement so one of them would finish art school, a pact that ended in love. She'd been expelled, but someone had to graduate. I'm exhausted. We've worked too hard.

I like staying with Lujo. The new house is wonderful. We light candles for glamour because blackouts are out of style.

"Thank God I'm not alone; I have tea and sympathy."

"Thank you, Papá. Lujo is a real luxury. Rest in peace. I release you—you deserve that," I say at sunset, already settled in front of the Malecón.

WORDS AGAINST OBLIVION

Lujo and I re-create Mami's show with her two "celebrity" announcers. Each tries to take the other's role. The theme: my mother's memory.

LUJO: What do you remember about your mother?

NADIA: What do you remember?

LUJO: First you and then me—c'mon . . .

NADIA: I remember her hand on my head, treating me for lice before I left for school. I was never early because my mother slept in. I would show up at recess. It was so embarrassing!

On the first of September they punished a group of six of us, and because I was the leader of the group, they demanded I come in with her the next day for a meeting. But she didn't want to. She hated listening to complaints. Especially about her daughter. Then she said, "Tell your teacher your mom says you're an orphan." I'll never forget the principal's face; that just made no sense. Nobody got it.

LUJO: What I remember is when an announcer didn't come in and your mother stayed to do his shift with me on Radio Reloj. She and I were so serious, reading those crazy news stories, one after the other. Then, half asleep, she said, "Today's Wednesday, March 20, 1978, and it's six thirty in the morning. Damn it, today's my birthday!" She cracked up laughing. They sent us both to hell.

NADIA: But, Lujo, my mom is my mother, right? Don't tell me I was picked up from a garbage can or some charity.

LUJO: You're so bad! Of course she's your mother.

NADIA: I remember the day your crazy announcer, Alina, said on the air, "María la Negra attacked the coasts of Angola," instead of "Black Tide attacked the coasts of Angola."

LUJO: The best was when Alina showed up at the studio saying, "Hey, folks, I have the record of the Concierto de Aranjuez played by Aranjuez himself." Your mother didn't know whether to laugh or kick her off the show. In a very serious tone, she asked her, "And what does he play?" And, as if out of her mind, Alina replied, "What's he going to play, sweetheart? The piano." *(They both laugh.)*

NADIA: Alina was as dumb as a rock, but Mami was clueless. She read and forgot commas, skipped letters. Once we were both hosting a children's program, and it was her turn to tell the story of Snow White. Mami tried to read it but didn't have her glasses and said, "Once upon a time there was a marriage without eyes." She was supposed to say "without *hijos*, without children." *(They both laugh.)*

LUJO: Do you remember "The girls from Havana are more than five hundred years old," instead of "The Walls of Havana"? She was so crazy! Nadia, the last time I saw you was in a cafeteria-bar called La Cibeles—you were dressed as a Pioneer. You were very small. It was daybreak and none of us had slept. We'd spent the night at a wake with some improv musicians. Then we went to drink at a bar. Your mother, who was a fan of their music, would not abandon the improvisers. One of the great Cuban improvisers had died.

NADIA: From the Buena Vista Social Club?

LUJO: Back then it was Mala Vista . . . The hungry old men who peed all over themselves and came drunk to the studio, asking for money, for cheap rum or moonshine. Your desperate mother would make coffee in the station's pantry so they could hold on and she could get them to sing one at a time. She was always so nervous, with her *Qui Êtes-Vous, Polly Maggoo?* hair. It was around that time when *Words Against Forgetting* began to air. People would call it "Words Against Our Ears" because no one could stand those old songs. Now the whole world has discovered the "martyrs of the son." But she's who left recordings of them. Really important stuff for the Cuban music history archive. Did you get a consultant fee when they came to talk to you?

NADIA: Imagine, my mother left all that with the station. You know she was obsessed with "posterity." Never mind the vulgarity of the day-to-day. If I'd ever collected a fee, I would've been going against her will, and the weight on my conscience wouldn't have let me sleep. In any case, she and my father were a couple of fools. They worked for others. She did it because she believed in that music, not for profit. Neither of them wanted money.

LUJO: Do you remember the day I saved you at the Pasacaballos Hotel?

NADIA: No, but I remember seeing you at the gymnastics competitions, cheering me on. What happened at the Pasacaballos?

LUJO: Taking advantage of a short break, she'd come from interviewing East German leader Erich Honecker and went to the hotel to pick up Ernesto Cardenal. This happened the same day and two hours apart. Nothing ever happens in this country, but when it happens, hold on, because it all happens at the same time. Taking advantage of a short break, your mother left you at the pool. When she got to the Cienfuegos station she called me: "Taking advantage of a short break—Oh, Lujo, for Marx's sake, for your mother's sake, I left the girl at the Pasacaballos." You can imagine, the Pasacaballos is a little far. But there went Uncle Lujo to rescue the girl. You were at peace, swimming alone in the middle of the night, floating in black waters. You looked like a jasmine flower carried by the current, from one side of the pool to the other, safe and floating like a tug in a port, waiting for someone who would never come back for you. Don't you remember me arguing with her about these things?

NADIA: No, what I remember is that she forgot to pick me up from school, so I spent hours with my teachers at their homes, waiting for her to come get me so I could shower, do my homework, and sleep. Never mind eating. It was just coffee with milk and bread and butter. She didn't know how to cook.

LUJO: She'd been troubled since that blow to the head at the coffee plantation, and then she got obsessed with work, which always came first for her.

NADIA: Yeah, we were secondary characters as far as our parents were concerned. That was back when a slogan was much more powerful than any emotion.

LUJO: Don't say that, Nadia, don't even kid about it.

NADIA: Look who's talking, the guy who didn't even try to have children.

LUJO: But I'm gay, girl.

NADIA: Like that means anything these days? How times change, Lujo Rojas!

LUJO: It's obvious they're never going to air these programs, Nadia Guerra!

NADIA: Before, you and my father were closeted about being a couple, and now see how you rationalize everything with your sexuality. And . . . now don't say anything. We're going to listen to Rubén González, to these *danzónes* my mom recorded for the program. Tell me, tell me if "El Cadete Constitucional" isn't something else when played by Rubén González's fabulous hands. Be quiet. Let's listen to this *danzón* for a while.

LUJO: If when walking someday through this or any other city in the world these sounds and words come back to you, remember you heard it here on a day like today, on this same station. Remember that these are words expressly pronounced "against oblivion."

THE BLACK BOX

Lujo and I have been standing at the exit door for two hours. Air France, the airline they were letting Mami fly, was late. She was in very poor health, fragile, whiny. It was the same state she was in when the Russian had sent her off from Moscow. With the airline's help, she made the connecting flight in Paris. She'd been stumbling for a long time. It's curious—she entered the country as a tourist and wasn't detained in immigration, but customs stopped her. The problem was ongoing. They let us in, and I see my mother in a wheelchair, tiny, nervous, crying. It hardly seems possible she's in Cuba with us now. The customs officer tries to explain something to me, but I'm not listening. I kiss my mother. She smells bad. There's food stuck to her face. She's peed herself. Her left hand trembles, her Parkinson's. God, what a state in which to come back. It's a very big deal to come back. What do I feel? Mostly anger, sick of so many absences. With me, with the sun here, the beach, with my father, maybe things would have been different. There are people who live in flight, who must leave where they're born. But there are beings so fragile that when they leave, the world swallows them whole. They get eaten up by the abstraction of traffic lights and accounts payable. Was that her case? I don't know; I don't know her.

The customs officer tells Lujo she refuses to open a cardboard box she's brought as her only luggage. She won't let them look at her papers either. I try to lift her from the wheelchair.

LUJO: Please give me your papers, your purse.
MAMI: My purse? What for? I don't have any money.
LUJO: Let's start with your papers.
MAMI: Take the papers, my purse, but not the box. Cuba took what's missing from that box. I never open it, never.

Lujo went pale. You don't mess around with customs; otherwise you can spend hours waiting for them to decide your fate and whether you get to leave the airport. The customs officer has his suspicions about this dirty, wheelchair-bound woman with a groggy face. They have suspicions about the box. They are suspicious because their job is to suspect, but the box holds only books with dust jackets that they don't even look at, some medicines, and documents. No money, no jewelry, no poison, no bombs. Nothing.

I ask them to run the box through the x-ray machine. They agree. The box is full of documents they want to read.

My mother is very ill. She trembles. They ask why she's trembling.

"It's Parkinson's," I tell them.

The customs officer doesn't care about the trembling madwoman in the wheelchair; she has to comply. Using his most courteous manners, he asks us to open the box. I open it. There's a photo of my mother when she was young. An article from *Bohemia* magazine at the beginning of the Revolution. The customs officer reaches inside the box. He can see typed pages. My mother, more lost than ever, screams, shrieks.

I WAS NEVER THE FIRST LADY

"My black box, my things! Leave them alone, damn it! Let go!"

The customs officer explains that you can't bring certain documents and books into Cuba. In her case, since she's sick, he thinks there won't be a problem. In any case, a specialist is coming to look over the books to be sure. Speaking slowly, he starts to tell her about the regulations . . . then my mother begins to sing in a powerful voice. It's "Words (*Palabras*)" by Marta Valdés:

> *Get away from me with your words,*
> *go find another heart that will welcome them.*

The tourists applaud; it is a hard spectacle to ignore. "This is Cuba, dude." The applause doesn't stop. The customs chief begs us to leave. My mother is rolled outside in her wheelchair. She kisses me although she doesn't recognize me. She hands Lujo the black box.

"And our husband, isn't he coming to meet me?" she asks Lujo. "Miami is so beautiful—finally, the sun!"

My mother doesn't know where she is, but she sang Marta Valdés imitating Elena Burke. She's here now, but now I don't know where to begin.

THE HOUSE, MY MOTHER, MEMORY, AND THE BODY

As soon as we got home, my mother began to ask about Lujo's mother. It was incredible, but she recognized the house in front of the Malecón. She remembered and listed certain phrases and things from when people used to come here to dance and pass the time:

1. The Beatles and other things were already banned.
2. We had already married our husband.
3. I was already pregnant with the girl.
4. Lujo's mother was on the couch.
5. I didn't paint anymore.
6. Waldo had been killed.
7. We weren't hippies anymore.
8. We didn't go to the Funeraria Park.
9. Nicolasito Guillén came over alone or with Dara, the Bulgarian.
10. Lujo's mother controlled who came and went.

Lujo sat down to read the medical history Mami brought along with her books. The documents suggested a degenerative disease of the central nervous system. Maybe Alzheimer's.

What kind of disease is this that retrieves then steals memories? The day we lose our memory is not the day memories are erased but only the day when we can't put them in order anymore or tie them to our emotions. Your loved ones start to become strangers to you. The intimate becomes alien. The day we lose our memory we're adrift.

Anything can save us or push us toward disaster. The enemy moves into your head.

THE BATH

I didn't know where to start. I began to undress her while she hummed in unison with Lujo. She couldn't finish a single song; she couldn't remember the lyrics all the way to the end, then she'd fall to earth like a kite from the sky.

I untangled some gauze on her thighs. I was trying to put her in the tub when I realized she had bedsores and scary bruises on her legs.

"She must have been lying or sitting a long time," said Lujo, appalled.

Mami was defiant and I almost had to force her under the soapy water; the sour smell of her body made us dizzy. She was skinny, malnourished. Lujo left the bathroom; he couldn't bear it. But my mother had no shame; she just went on singing, naked.

After your memory goes, everything else follows: shame, modesty, fear. But candor comes back.

I sponged her onion skin. She was no more than fifty-five years old but so fragile . . . She almost melted between the water and foam. She'd once had a beautiful body.

In the bathtub, she played with the soaps and bottles, like a little girl. I couldn't help a few tears; I don't know why I couldn't keep it together in these first few minutes alone with her. "Control, Nadia," I tell myself, terrified. I ask her about the bruises.

"The person who takes care of me in Russia is an animal. She beats me."

I wanted to run away, but I breathed, I kept calm.

"But why, Mami? Were you left alone with her? What did you do?"

"I don't know. I didn't misbehave. I swear I've been good."

I didn't cry again. I don't know how I feel about my mother; it could be I haven't had time to figure things out for myself yet. But the thing is, I didn't cry again. I didn't know if she was lying or if she actually remembered any of the things she said.

Lujo shows me how to take care of the bedsores. First, you have to put on gloves, but I don't have gloves. I disinfect my hands with alcohol, then clean the wounds with hydrogen peroxide. I put alcohol on them immediately and my mother jumps, slaps my hand. I kiss her to calm her down, then I put antibiotic cream on her, letting my fingers sink into the sores. I make the medicine penetrate to the bone; at the end, I blot them a bit. I blow on the wounds so there's no burning, and then we're done. It took a little bit of time for each one . . . and now the worst is over.

Lujo shows me how to help her put on the disposable diapers she brought. My mother watches us from the bed. I use some Brisa talcum, which I'd forgotten about and left on the dresser since the '80s. I dab a little of my perfume and deodorant on her and dress her in my pajamas. I comb her hair, and she's ready to have dinner, to sleep, to be quiet at home. At whose house?

"At home," Lujo says, starting to fall apart.

Lujo cries while looking for a Bola de Nieve LP. We hear "Goodbye Happiness" from the Hungarian record player that sits in a corner of the room. This is the place I'll share with my mom until we know what to do in the future. Is there a future without memory?

Lujo knows and loves my mother more than I do. The sobs startle her awake. I feel a lot of guilt, but now isn't the time for blame. I can't cry for her—that's not what she expects from me. My mother has fallen asleep again, and Lujo has gone to make smoothies for the three of us. I want to take a shower; I'm exhausted. I look at myself in the mirror, naked. I have the same body as my mother's.

As I wash, I release a few hysterical tears. I turn off the water; I close my eyes. End of hysteria. Enough, enough, enough already. End of the day.

I go to be by my mother, who's like a little girl lost between the sheets; she breathes calmly. Everything is at peace except me: "A stranger has come / To share my room in the house not right in the head, / A girl mad as birds," said Dylan Thomas.

THE ORWO TAPE

I find an Orwo tape (recorded in Havana, 1980) in my mother's box. I listen to it on the Nagra tape recorder. This is like being in a museum, with a little of everything.

SOUNDTRACK: *Tap, tap, tap . . . on the open microphone. A hand taps again, three times.*

Do you hear me, skinny girl?

It's four in the morning. I'm at the station, in front of the RCA Victor in the green sound booth. You know I don't like listening to my recorded voice—I feel like it sounds watered down—but this is the only chance I have to speak to you. There's nobody here and the microphone's visible, tangible, not hidden. I'm recording myself so I can be sure. I can't leave you a letter, and a drawing wouldn't let me fit in everything I'm thinking. I'm not a genius; I'm just your mom.

I hope your father hands you this tape someday. It's not urgent, and I'd rather he give it to you when you're older. I won't come back—I don't think they'll let me, and I don't think I'll let myself.

Today, if they were to catch me recording this tape at the station, they would sanction me, fire me, interrogate me, send me far away until they've forgotten my mistakes. I could wind up at Topes de Collantes. But that's the least of it right now. My head is spinning. I'm trying to say goodbye to you.

When you grow up and hear this, maybe over there *(coughs)* . . . By the year 2000, this will be a different life. I hope scientific breakthroughs and the human condition will have overcome all the meanness of humankind. Then you can listen to this as a relic from the past and you won't understand anything; you'll listen from a distance, in the same way that today we listen to radio soap operas like *The Right to Be Born*. I'll be history, or worse, I'll be nothing at all, and nobody will forgive me for leaving you behind, for leaving without you; that's the honest living truth—don't think I'm ignoring it. I'm well aware of it.

I'm in the sound booth where we spent so many hours together, me with my white glass and you with your chiseled silver spoon. Here we drank tea amidst all those ants. Here we ate what we could. Here we gossiped about men, about friends. We read poems we liked and laughed at a few with Aleida and Maricela as well. Here I answered what I could of your questions. Here you slept on the sofa, exhausted, still wearing your school uniform, waiting for my shift to end at dawn, during cyclones and political events. But I don't want to start lying to you here. It's time you know I don't agree with everything that's happening to us. It's time for you to know I'm leaving.

SOUNDTRACK: *The sound of a spoon stirring sugar into liquid in a glass.*

Several months ago your father found a new woman. A twenty-four-year-old girl who's a reporter for the official newspaper. She's a recent graduate and writes news and opinion pieces. Sometimes she thinks she has our country in her hands. One day she'll figure out who's allowed to have opinions and who has the last word on this island.

Well, my love, let me get to it . . . She came into our house and ransacked it, stole my diaries, a novel about that friend I've told you about. The one who just died. She revealed the secret you and I shared.

The novel has vanished, and now there are questions at work. They call me, they ask me for reports, they ask me questions I don't understand and that are going to drive me crazy, Nadia.

Staying would be detrimental to you and your father. I've always been the black sheep, the madwoman, the deranged. They censor your father, but they let him go on making movies. They won't tolerate me. They can't forgive me for who I am. There are people watching me at every turn.

Although it's not always easy to see, they persecute me. I feel them; they're here. There are eyes watching me everywhere. A lot has happened at home over the past few weeks. Posters with our names accompanied by profanities went up. The orange notebook we loved was burned at our front door. They threw your grandfather's antique table down the stairs, broke it. That's why I sent you to be with Aleida, so you wouldn't get upset.

Your father's ex-lover is the spearhead of the mystery; she's been promoted very quickly at that official newspaper. Lover of politicians and leaders. Unique, tough to beat. She's the daughter or granddaughter of a minister—I'm not sure— but she's got lots of license and has no scruples and doesn't care about your age or our life plans . . . I've complained, but nobody listens to me.

I've thought about publicly protesting, saying it loud . . . but why bother? Actually, we can't really fight against that sort of thing. It's like trying to knock down the Berlin Wall. These are cruelties you all will have to eliminate someday. With force. From "a world more just than yesterday's world," as your school song goes.

I can't do anything here anymore. They've kicked me out, they've won . . . I'm leaving.

There are a ton of anonymous notes and letters she and your father wrote each other. It's all very vulgar. What was secret is now exposed. It makes me sick. Our lives are now open to everyone—impossible for a woman like me.

All this scares me, my girl, it scares me *(heavy breathing)*. Photos of your father and me left ripped up by the front door, handfuls of salt, red ribbons—I don't understand anything. Shit on the walls in the foyer. Witchcraft, eggs, objects I don't recognize. Private conversations I've had with your father later reproduced at public assemblies, on this station—anyway, a nightmare, the perfect plot, like the movie *Rosemary's Baby, La semilla del diablo*. Whatever you want to call it, this looks like a Polanski film.

Nadia, if you ever want to come be with me, you'll be welcomed. I've never been a good mother. I'm a great friend who gave you the opportunity to come into this world and to know there's another. That's where I'm headed. If it doesn't beat me, I'll reclaim you, and if it does, I want you to know I do all this for you. I don't want to mark you; I don't want you to be stigmatized because of me.

I love you, my skinny girl, and I'll always be broadcasting on this frequency for you.

Listen to the *soneros*, the bolero players, go with your father to hear the troubadours, they live and sing, listen to what they say. They're the greatest thing on this island, my love. And I want you to know something: This is not your mom and dad's revolution. This is just a *big misunderstanding*.

(Tearful.) Skinny girl, I want you to be better than us, but I can't help you with that. Your father is a weak man; he doesn't even know how to defend his own talent. I'm leaving because I'm shattered and I can't help you by going on in this condition.

A huge kiss.

Hopefully I can rewrite the novel about our friend. Why do they fear a tribute to someone so clean and admirable?

Someday you'll see it published and then you'll know your mother did nothing wrong. Nothing worse than abandoning you . . . *(silence)*, because of this fear that overwhelms me.

I already saw the Camejo puppets on fire at the Guiñol; they've already expelled me from art school for being homosexual (though I'm not); they've already accused me of loving foreign things; they've separated me from those whom I've loved the most. Enough, enough, my skinny girl! I don't want that for me or you. I'm going to hold my head up high in the real world, in the jungle.

How will everything be in 2000? I hope better than today. That's what all this sacrifice is for . . . Make sure it's not in vain. Nadia, I quit. I can't take it anymore, my little daughter. You, go on.

Remember these things:

If your nose bleeds, throw your head back and stay calm.

If you get lost, call the station; everyone here knows you and they'll take you back home.

Never tell on anyone, no matter what. Don't cry for no reason; there'll always be an excuse.

Don't fall in love with someone who doesn't deserve you. I'm saying this from experience.

Don't miss me. There's no need; I'll always be with you.

I'm going to stop giving you advice and go. My girl, we're a couple of disasters, your parents. I hope your father stays with you until the end. In the worst-case scenario, there's a list of friends who know about this. I know nothing will happen to you.

Don't stop looking for me when you're older, and I'll do the same, no matter what happens.

I love you so much, my long-haired girl. You're a piece of me, of Cuba . . . I'll carry you with me. I'll miss you from this moment on. I've recorded this song for you. Don't forget it. Learn it by heart. We are both entwined in this music.

SOUNDTRACK: *Steps and then the noise of a door opening and closing, then a sound as the tape disconnects.*

SOUNDTRACK: *The song "If It Weren't for You (*Si No Fuera Por Ti*)" by Pedro Luis Ferrer starts immediately.*

> *If it weren't for you*
> *and your faith in things . . .*

RED DIARY

Now I understand my mother's poems. And I increasingly understand my obsession with radio. I was left in the care of the radio. That's nuts! Now radio is in me. I walk alone, trying to put together, out of nowhere, this sound puzzle.

I'm facing this black cardboard box, having surrendered to the penance of the past. The worst part is confirming that, even in 2006, things are still unknown. Nothing's been solved; everything runs like sand through our hands. I understand my mother's motives, and the wrongful testimonies given by her witnesses. I copy the poems she wrote at the station, looking for clues. I'm her spare memory.

NOTES IN THE MARGINS OF A PHOTOGRAPH

Do you remember, Aleida, the story of the frog photo?
We didn't know then we were happy, when in the
real photo you, my daughter, and Maricela showed
your kindest faces. Time gilds and beautifies images,

but I know, I'm sure, we were quite a little gang at the assemblies. We weren't nice to our detractors; we had no mercy.

That's why they'll never forget us, even if they leave room for a little gall along with the memories.

But here's the photo: Maricela, you, and my daughter, champions of the dead words that now keep us so distant from each other.

The sun hits you in the face, and my daughter narrows her brow until she squints. Maricela borrows her mother's expression, lost in a vision of gypsies who come through childhood in a caravan, and you, like in that tormenting story about the frog, you don't know how to hide your deep joy; your face can't do it. Take care, Aleida, so that nothing ever shuts down that look, that laugh, that it may always be a constant sound in your ears.

RARE AND VALUABLE
COLLECTIONS

I listened to the Orwo tape without saying a word. I couldn't cry. I just lay down next to my mother, curled up with her, apologized for not understanding her.

I keep looking in the box with curiosity, reading documents from this messy attempt at research for a novel and a lost life. My mother randomly stitched her fragmented ideas together. I remember afternoons with her at the library. I had just learned to read the big poster: "Rare and Valuable Collections" department. She fished for clues through loose papers, for ideas for her lost novel.

I listen to the tape several times, which keeps going around in the deluxe recorder until it gets tangled and stops abruptly. My mother wakes up, looks at me, scared, and closes her eyes again. I kiss her.

"Who are you?" she asks, exhausted.

"It's me, Mami. Your daughter."

"I don't want to meet new people. I already have quite a lot with those I know."

Now I cry. I want to close my eyes, take ten of her pills, and not wake up until I've forgotten everything. I want to be blank and not think about what's happened to us.

Dear Diego:
I need you.

My mother is finally here. Lujo and I went to pick her up at the airport. The trip has affected her. She seems worse to me than during my visit to Russia. They put her in a wheelchair the minute she landed. She had no luggage; she's wearing my clothes now. She arrived completely crazy, hugging a cardboard box and a Chanel purse with seven books with homemade jackets, very little money, and all her documents (Russian, Cuban, and French).

Her mind has stopped working. Lujo and I cradle her like a little girl. I don't know if you're traveling outside Mexico. I need to talk. Tell me when that can happen. I'm dying just seeing her like this. She forgot Lujo, and she speaks to me as if she's never seen me before.

The few hours she manages to sleep, she curls up, frightened, in the bed. I can't believe she's here. I don't know what Lujo did to get her here, but she's with us.

I adore you. Help, I'm drowning.

Nadia

WHO AM I?

Someone has plans for me, and the worst part is that I don't know. Three men in white rolled-up shirts open and close their hands at the same time. They're here to donate blood. I see very tight, café-au-lait-colored garters strangling their arms until the blood flow is cut and sterile cotton wool scorches their skin. Two dry taps of the nurse's fingers means the needle's coming; it goes in rigorously until I feel it at the blue point of my origin. The blood splatters into the syringe, and then everything is red and thick.

We are in the sterile act of investigation. Who am I and why are they preparing this exhaustive exam? They drive into my flesh: it burns, it hurts, I feel empty, and then they give me back my arm and gather my genetic information. They give my "self" a coagulating agent. The nurse asks why I don't complain.

"I don't feel anything anymore," I say as I roll down my sleeves and leave with no particular place to go.

All the suspects have given permission to get pinched. Each at a different point on the planet. Lujo is a frustrated soap opera writer and is determined to find out who my father is. I could not care less. My father is and will always be the same man; I don't want another. He made me who I am, lowered my fevers, saw me cry, menstruate, love, leave, leave again. I don't believe in anyone else. The imprecise thing is that I still can't quite say: "This is my father; this is my country; this is my mother; this is my home."

MAY 28

My dearest Nadia:

I returned to Milan from Zurich yesterday and spoke with Paolo B. I brought him my father's will; he's the only lawyer my father trusts since he left Cuba. Once we finished that business, we talked about you.

Paolo told me something related to you and yours that I think will touch you very deeply, especially given what you're going through right now. Get ready for that. He's going to Cuba with the sole purpose of speaking to you.

Your mother's impoverishment is no surprise, and although it's cruel, you have to accept it. Don't let Paolo B.'s news bring you down. As soon as you need me, call me.

It was dusk when we finished talking and, on my way home along the semi-snowy Alps, I wondered if I had been happy when I was a reporter in this part of the world, if I really enjoyed that stage, seeing the wondrous, windy Alps out my window, traveling all over Europe, being paid to do what I'd always dreamed of. Why do vanity and the desire for notoriety and pseudo-transcendence always take precedence? I can't be more aware of how privileged I've been. Fate has provided me with an uncommon life, but I insist on worrying about trivialities at work. Lately I've had insomnia, working nonstop without rest.

It doesn't matter what I get out of it. I'm as bad a winner as I am nefarious a loser. If something doesn't go well, I find it difficult to accept defeat; if something goes well, I'm an even worse winner, because the euphoria passes and I'm off, already thinking about the next goal. I might be a kind of insatiable predator, although, evidently, my prey is either insufficient or hidden and doesn't always come my way. The result: permanent frustration.

It's not fair, Nadia. There's so much to worry about in the world, and so many people burdened with terrible situations. And then there are the lucky ones, a legion, convinced that our sorrows and anxieties are indeed heavy. We know little and understand even less. I send you many kisses. I know I don't deserve this beauty. I want to share it with you, but it's still not the right time for you.

I share your pain, and every day I sleep with you and love you.

Your Diego

Part III

MY MOTHER'S UNFINISHED BOOK

(FRAGMENTS FOUND IN THE BLACK BOX)

MEETING CELIA

I stared at the wooden house on stilts: the pines, the taro, the bugs . . . There was no one in the house; they'd left for Miami because they didn't approve of what was happening to the country. Leaving me and my sister was supposed to be provisional. We'd come to live with that unusual condition and, without realizing it, being on our own had turned into forever.

I was alone and decided to use my time painting everything; with our parents gone, the house would be lost to us. I wanted to leave my mark. Without the slightest forethought, I started on the white linoleum floor. Using a Chinese pen, I inked soft autumn leaves, bells, black cherries, umbrellas, high heels, clovers, golf clubs, moons. They made the impeccable surface shine, the one we'd praised so much last Christmas.

For the first time, I felt free—without the obligations of the American school, or Christian efforts on Sundays, or the daily despair of my mother, awake until four or five in the morning and standing at the door waiting for my father to return from the Guantánamo Bay Naval Base. I painted walls, doors, furniture, counteracting the strange sensation of liberation and orphanhood provoked by the emptiness.

My sister, fantasizing about our parents' almost impossible return, couldn't stop laughing while imagining their shoes on the floor tiles, their surprise at seeing my careful and profuse drawings. A house illustrated with incongruous figures.

My sister had been taken to Tía Dora's chalet before, which was on the corner, very close by. They wanted to convince her of what they could never convince me, but she was firm and came back immediately to be with me; Digna, our Black nanny, ran back and forth from one house to the other, trying to attend to two rebellious girls. Digna, in fact, had always taken care of us, but this world was ending for us, and no one was able to intervene at all.

A different life began for us; the previous one didn't exist anymore. A good life, making our own decisions and eating, from time to time, what little we found in the cupboards.

I said I would stay to work on the literacy campaign, that I'd go be with our parents later. I was only fourteen years old, but I was interested in more than just working for a company. Later I could study in the United States. I didn't want to harangue like a Quaker or Protestant minister (which was, in fact, what my parents wanted for me). When the '60s caught us in their whirlwind, all those projects went nowhere.

My sister stayed with me, but not out of conviction. She was sixteen years old. We became members of the Conrado Benítez Brigade, but we worked on the literacy project in different areas. She wasn't trained for the life she was leading, and from what I could tell, she volunteered for whatever popped up. That's a trait of hers I like a lot, something I don't share: she's adaptable, doesn't complain, and she thinks the best is yet to come.

The day we went to hear Fidel at the plaza, we were both chosen to go to the Habana Libre Hotel to meet a group of journalists who wanted to interview us.

While we were standing in line, a very delicate woman discreetly approached me and asked if we'd been to Varadero, enjoying some time as a reward for our work on the literacy campaign. Standing by her, and almost in a whisper, I told her that no, we'd had to go to Banes, to close the family home and gather our documents. My parents had left the country, and we'd had to divide things up and come here.

The woman gave some thought to my story. She led me out of the tumult with two escorts, then we looked for the brigade to which my sister belonged. We left in a car as we heard Fidel's hoarse voice come on the speakers. We went through the Habana Libre lobby with two militiamen guiding us, asking everyone to move along.

I liked the place. It was a hotel built in the '50s, carpeted and luxurious. I looked in the mirrors, breathed in the air-conditioning and the smell of French perfume and fine pastries. We went up in a silver elevator, and when the suite doors opened, Celia—Celia Sánchez—appeared with her back to us, looking at something on a dresser she was using as a desk.

I stared at her, unable to avoid the embarrassment typical of us girls from the countryside.

The slim guerrilla wore black sandals and a light yellow dress. She had gathered her long and straight black hair with a ribbon of the same color. She looked like a Greek sculpture and welcomed us calmly, smiling.

Suddenly my sister and I were at the very center of a crowd with Celia, but we didn't have a clue what was going on. Then all three of us were subjected to an unstoppable barrage of picture-taking.

Why us? We weren't better or worse than the other literacy teachers in the plaza with Fidel. The answer to the question of why we were there would come to me later: history doesn't always privilege the heroic; what's at hand can also be seen as epic.

Those photos would later appear in newspapers and reach Miami. My father's reaction was "Turn off the lights," but portrayed in black and white in our literacy campaign uniforms, we were delighted with our lives. What a contradiction! The sisters, Americans born in Cuba (or better, in a part of Cuba that isn't Cuba, at the Guantánamo Bay Naval Base), were now fighting, along with everyone else, against imperialism.

Subtly, Celia asked the photographers to leave. She didn't seem to like the spectacle.

My sister hugged me very sparingly and stiffly, like a stick, which is her way.

"Did you already kiss Celia?" she asked.

I shook my head, and she pushed me toward Celia. As I kissed her, I sniffed a perfume I'd never smell again. I was trembling. I couldn't help it. Celia asked me if anything was wrong.

"I need to pee," I managed to say.

Then she led me to a large, lighted bathroom, which was more like a bedroom, and waited for me to come out. My sister told her she was going to study medicine. She wanted to be a pathologist. Intrigued, Celia asked why pathology. My sister said she intended to save lives only by working under the microscope; she didn't like patients.

"I'd rather be among the dead and a bunch of tumors than among the living who complain all the time," she added resolutely, and Celia was very amused with her comment.

Then she asked if I was interested in studying anything in particular.

"I want to go to art school," I said. "I like to paint."

She asked if we'd seen exhibitions. I explained how little I knew about all that: the Bacardí Museum, *Selecciones* magazine, *The Youth Treasure* encyclopedia, and a small museum of pre-Columbian art in Banes. She gave me a thick, two-color pencil, one of those red and blue ones, and pulled the curtains so I could draw on the wall.

"Draw something," she said.

Something of mine? I hadn't a thought. My elbow trembled; my pulse felt tight; I was afraid everything would turn out disasterously.

"Relax, girl," said my sister.

Celia was smiling, delighted.

I made a sketch with no apparent shape, and then, as if by magic, it turned into a woman with a bird's head. Celia said no one would erase that bird from the wall; I was so nervous I hadn't noticed there were other people in the room with us.

When she got a phone call, I entertained myself by looking out the giant window. Havana was a gem. I loved the buildings and the sea at sunset—everything was like new. Celia stared like a child at that bird with a woman's body that I had released into the room.

My sister and I said our goodbyes. But Celia didn't let us go back to the plaza. She was worried about us, asked where we would sleep that night. She had other questions, none that offended us. (The woman from the plaza had told her our story.) Celia didn't mention Miami or our parents. We would stay with the other literacy workers, she said, and a while later she asked us to get in a jeep that would take us to her house in El Vedado.

First, we waited for the rally to end. It was impossible to

get through the sea of people coming down Twelfth Street from the plaza. Celia drove frowning, her long arms and sleeves draped over the wheel. While we waited at the traffic lights, she glanced down at a folder full of papers on her lap. Her sandaled feet worked the pedals.

At her house, she introduced us to two women, Pucha and Mary. They took care of us and gave my sister and me towels, soap, and identical pajamas.

They dabbed us with violet water and led us to bunk beds ready with sheets that smelled clean.

We ended up having chicken soup and drank milk from white enamel mugs. I think that's why I love mugs. That night I didn't get even two hours' sleep. My heart was fluttering.

"If Mom finds out about this, she'll come back from Miami and sign up for a militia. But Dad will have a coronary," said my sister.

Everyone in our family knew who Celia's father was; they knew Celia too. My mom adored Frank País, and Frank País adored Celia. Because of that, and because of Radio Rebelde, we knew about her and that she was the bravest of them all, and that they had been looking to kill her. My mom had seen her once in Manzanillo, but she didn't talk about it because my dad hated everything that had to do with revolutionaries.

I got up and went to the kitchen to see if I could get a glass of water, half for my sister and half for me. The others were sound asleep. I later learned they'd come with Celia from the Sierra. They were sick of seeing the same things. But not us.

I ran the water through the filter, and when I least expected it, two cars parked just below the kitchen window and lit up the whole house. Everyone woke up. It was Fidel. I didn't see him, but it was him. I knew from the sound of his boots, people coming through the door, and the noise and whispers of the women who attended us.

Celia was sitting halfway up the stairs, pen in hand. She saw me in the hallway and greeted me with a wink while she waited, dressed in white, misty clothes; she was barefoot. She waved goodbye, and I ran back into the bedroom. So scary!

My sister was also listening to the cars and wanted me to tell her I'd seen Fidel.

"Tell me, even if it's a little lie."

"No, I didn't see him, but if she was waiting and there was all this running around, who else could it be?"

My sister and I fell asleep in our bunks. We were more alone than anyone in this world. We didn't know the people whose house we were at, but that day, we felt like part of their family.

I wonder where the others who were there that day are now. What happens to things that excite us but get so seriously watered down it isn't worthwhile to remember them? That's when we're silent, but do we actually forget?

For example, my sister barely remembers any of this. I ask her if she forgets just to bug me or if she really has forgotten everything. I don't think there's an answer to that. I don't even know how many days we stayed there. We met many comandantes, soldiers, and people related to La Sierra who came and went, including this family. It was like we were in a movie.

I went on to study painting at the Escuela Nacional de Arte, officially entering on January 15, 1962, and my sister enrolled in pre-med at the medical school. The schools were close so we saw each other during breaks; she came to the ENA or I stayed over in her dorm. Months passed, and Celia seemed like a dream to us. My sister and I never talked about it. We were Daughters of the Homeland, minors, so we couldn't go out alone, not even on weekends. Sometimes during the holidays they let our classmates' families take us home with them.

At the art school, I met almost everyone who is now among my closest friends. The craziest, most distracted, creative, delusional, and even normal people.

It was a blast to hang out with Amarilis and Waldo Luis, lying on the grass on the old golf course, looking at the lost moon through firebricks and talking sublime nonsense. That's when I understood I wasn't alone in the world, that I belonged to a special place with enlightened and marginalized beings. People who'd been integrated or excluded and who, like me, brought their own madness and insisted on the same outbursts and sadness. They weren't there to study but to try to heal and, once they finished painting, to try to heal those who would see their works, because maybe art could repair their spirits as well.

We were like broken mirrors rebuilding one another. By ourselves we'd never be able to reflect anything. That was how I realized I could collect the parts of myself I was missing. Going there was the only way to get inside myself.

Celia herself left us at the bus stop by the beach and indicated where my sister and I should go. My sister left on the medical school bus. I walked until I saw the scaffolding going up to build the domes, a budding castle opening before the country club, which would be my home for several years.

Little by little, the master plan became reality. The school has a wonderful design. Seen from above, from a high point like the red-brick bell tower, you can distinguish the figure of a naked woman, and in the long curve that makes up the domes and the visual arts classrooms, you can see a fountain that depicts the moist sex of a woman asleep on the old country club lawn.

There wasn't enough material to paint and study, and the buildings weren't finished yet. The architects Porro, Garatti, and Gottardi, one Cuban and the others Italian, roamed the school until late at night.

Sometimes Celia called, asking about me; I know this because some professors told me, but never the principal, a tyrant who imposed military discipline: painters marching to the dining room, dancers marching to the bathroom. Madness.

In the first months a collective call was made to join the mobilization to harvest coffee in the eastern zone. On December 22nd, in the Plaza de la Revolución, we asked Fidel: "Tell us what else we can do. We will always do our duty." And Fidel answered: "Harvest coffee"—and we took off for the mountains.

I actually wanted to be in Havana. But I couldn't—and I didn't want to—miss this new adventure. In any case, no one was staying behind at the school. I would have preferred to read and paint, but we'd asked Fidel and he'd given his answer.

Apparently this was part of the economic struggle being waged as a result of the Second Declaration of Havana. I don't know, at the time nobody was asking too many questions; we put everything away where we could and went off to the hills.

My luggage was a cardboard box. We went on a train, different schools mixed together, boys and girls together, but I don't remember where my sister was at the time. The journey seemed to never end, but we finally arrived in Guantánamo, near the base where I was born. I remembered my mother, cried a few tears, and made a sketch of her face in my notebook. I didn't want to forget it. I knew our family was now the whole world, but my mother's face was my mother's face, and that was no game. For me, this was indeed a journey in reverse.

My God, we were so hungry! I missed the scholarship-funded meals the high-life chef used to cook, substituting spices with whatever he had on hand. We used to call those meals "Whatever's not gone with the wind." I missed my mattress, the school cafeteria, the fine cutlery with which we had learned how to eat in a refined way, the people who returned to visit after they'd left in the '60s. We were living in their mansions, located around the club, full of encyclopedias, stylish furniture, fine ornaments—we had destroyed it all. We hadn't known what to do with what we found in the drawers or on the shelves of those houses; we couldn't even imagine what or how half those implements were used.

We waited all morning at the park in Guantánamo, and in the end, all fourteen visual arts students were sent to Santo Domingo de Sagua. We were exhausted by the time we arrived. It was so muddy they had to tie the truck to tree trunks with a steel cable. I was terrified of the precipice, the emptiness. "The abyss calls the abyss."

Finally, we came to a large tent with a zinc roof near the Toa River; it had a coffee-drying room. It was El Achiotal, where Raúl Castro had founded the Second Front in the Sierra Cristal. We ate boiled mushrooms and Russian meat. We passed a farmhouse where there was a small store, which would later supply us with groceries, and a very nice wooden house where a French family lived.

We made the journey singing revolutionary songs, boleros, and laments. Although we weren't lost, it wasn't a very accessible place either, and that worried me a lot. I'm one of those people who always have a map in their heads with the fire exits marked, just in case.

I fell fast asleep in a stick hut where several girls were assigned to live together, with hammocks and all sorts of junk. When I woke up, I realized the back part of the hut had a kitchen covered with royal palm leaves and a latrine I never used because, in those cases, I've always preferred the outdoors.

We met the chief, the owner of the stick hut. An unbearable man. He lived there with his wife, María, and two boys. His biblical name, Adonai, comes and goes from my memory of him giving orders.

"You have to work from daybreak until night falls! If you don't work, there's no food! You pay for your food with your work!"

None of us knew how to pick coffee. At this point nobody wanted to be there.

We got up at half past five in the morning. Amarilis, the skinny one, cried and cried. We drank María's watery coffee. The days and nights there erased any desire to paint, read, or even sing. We were only aware that the ditches we dug were called furrows. Backpacks on our shoulders, we learned to shred the bushes without damaging the green grains. It wouldn't stop raining; it was as if the sky was crying all day. Every Sunday, a little sunshine peeked out. We were hungry and cold. I got bored of mushrooms and weeds boiled in a bucket.

To drive away the bibijagua ants, which sneaked in between our waist and navel, we smeared ourselves with kerosene. I'll hate that smell the rest of my life. We were short, so we got lost among the old, tall coffee plants in the folds of the hills. The ground was muddy, and I often slipped, anchoring my boots against the tree trunks so as not to fall.

Coffee Plantation Shelter

Ancient legends
from the coffee plantations
conspire against us.
In the middle of the night
the sounds of
a lost mule's bell.
Who knows
where it stopped,
resigned and terrified,
before the short-necked
duck's macabre teasing?
Laughter's mightier
than any legend.
It's us, compañeras,
waking the day among the leaves
and the coffee beans,
yawning the last yawn of the night.
The cold, fatigue,
the coffee mug passed from mouth to mouth

makes us of a piece.
Coffee plantation shelter,
the warm arm of a woman
against which silence collapses.

One day, while looking over a cliff, what I had imagined happened: I lost my balance and was left hanging by my backpack. At first I almost hanged myself and then I rolled down a steep slope, hitting myself against all sorts of things, and saw the vegetation and the mud in a circular way, like from a porthole, until a rock brought my head to a stop and I lost my senses, my balance, and my memory. At this point in history, I think it was the best thing that could've happened to me.

From that moment on, from that time on, what I remember most is the bitter sweetness deep inside the red coffee beans; the night swims in a stream of icy black water; Marisol—the group's philosopher, who stayed on shore to keep her promise not to wash up until she got back to the ENA—and the look on her face.

The moment I felt the blow, I let go. I abandoned this world, which didn't seem like a bad plan. It was Marisol who went with me to the hospital. According to what I was later told, I was taken to Havana. I survived being carried from one car to another until I finally arrived, alive, at the hospital.

I saw images between fainting spells, as if everything happened far away, outside of me. I vaguely remember being moved from a truck. According to Marisol, there was a column of barefoot militiamen, like a dream of what had been described on Radio Rebelde a few years earlier about the struggle in the Sierra. Something important was happening now with the militia. Marisol thought it might have been raids against bandits. Maybe other rebels, other insurgents, were in the hills, but no. Later, in the hospital, she told me we were on the verge of war. All those mobilized men remained in the mountains.

Back in camp, the girls got tired of picking what was no longer there, but they were trapped in the same surreal story out on the hills.

Havana was tense. Marisol said US ships could be seen near the coasts. War tanks were parked on the Malecón; there were trenches, sandbags, and armed people everywhere.

I felt bad for Marisol, who sometimes slept in the bed with me, or on the iron rocking chair in the hospital room. But she didn't complain: "So long as I'm in Havana," she said, "I don't care if we're at war or if I'm in an operating room."

I don't remember the operation, and I don't want to talk about it. I'd rather forget those things. The cures, the pain, and the consequences are buried deep in my memory. Ready to be forgotten. My head was shaved; I looked like a girl from the Middle Ages, one of those bald girls I'd seen in book illustrations.

One day, asleep and still troubled, I opened my eyes. Who was at the head of my bed? Celia, my sister, and Pucha. I couldn't believe it. I hadn't remembered my sister until then. I hadn't asked about her. What was happening with my memory? I felt guilty.

Celia, without a word, placed birds of paradise in an earthenware vase next to my bed. I kissed all three of them very dramatically and started crying like a fool.

"I don't have time for crybabies," Celia said. "Much less to sit here and pat your hand and tell you it'll be okay. I'll leave you with your sister, who's been looking everywhere for you."

Pucha put a notebook and a yellow pencil on the table, along with a new pencil sharpener and a very fragrant eraser.

"If you get out of this alive, we're going to organize a show of your work," my sister said, trying to be a smarty-pants, "but first we have to get through what's happening out there."

Celia didn't say anything. She kissed me and told me to take care of myself. I told her better she take care of herself. I noticed her eyes were restless. She said goodbye and practically ran out the door.

Pucha said goodbye too and stopped a nurse who was pushing Celia, already at the door. My sister, Marisol, and I were surprised because the nurse never recognized Celia.

My sister had been vainly tracking Celia, who was virtually invisible, whether on TV or in the newspapers. Finally she'd found her at the door to the house on Once Street, and together they'd found the hospital.

My sister kept giving me advice. I knew something was going on in my head and in Cuba. The good thing was we'd found each other again and we couldn't believe it. My schoolmates came down from the mountains three months later, when someone thought to send for them at the end of the crisis. They graduated in 1967, the first class of artists from the school Fidel created. I didn't graduate, I was expelled, but that's a story I'll tell another time. My head is more or less okay. Unfortunately, my memory is intact.

CELIA, BROOKLYN,
AND SNOW

As a young woman, Celia suffered from hives that became more frequent and severe. Her family decided to send her to New York, where her brother Orlando lived, to undergo tests and treatments. The tests confirmed the Cuban doctors' diagnosis: she was allergic to almost everything but mango.

After she got her prescriptions, the girl was so inquisitive about the city that, even after Orlando saw the hives were under control, he asked her not to go back to Cuba until she'd had a chance to experience snow. She stayed in New York six months.

Her brother and Julio Girona, a Cuban painter from Manzanillo, were close friends. As a result, Julio's sisters became Celia's fairy godmothers, although, in fact, they were distantly related, which they always joked about when they got together. The Girona sisters showed Celia the city. They say she seemed like a curious child, snooping, discovering fascinating facts in that endless world. She wrote everything down, absorbed everything she saw around her. She visited as many museums as she could because, as she said, "her taste for art was inborn."

She frequented public libraries and met and talked with

immigrants on the street, asking questions, whether she was out alone or with others. She was very daring and loved to set out to discover the unknown.

She was fascinated by Chinatown and the way the merchants displayed their merchandise. They let her joke around in Spanish, without understanding her Cuban jokes or gestures. She took pictures in front of the statue of José Martí and walked through the streets he'd traveled during his New York days. She enjoyed a quick getaway to Niagara Falls. She loved to ride on the ferry. She thought a lot when she was alone and yet felt accompanied by this new family. Although it had been a bad year for her family, and for her in particular, in 1948 New York, Celia was happy.

The Gironas convinced Orlando to move closer to them, and they eventually ended up as neighbors: 97 Clark Street, Brooklyn.

One afternoon, it snowed. She and Orlando were at a neighborhood theater watching a Mexican movie. At the end of the showing, just as they were leaving the theater, snowflakes settled on the girl's head. She sat down on a park bench, shivering as her eyes surveyed the small universe within her sight. Little by little, the whiteness enveloped her. It was, at last, snow. Snow that melts with a breath, as ephemeral as flowers and the illusion of love, but which, like flowers and illusions, is remembered for a lifetime. As she looked at herself, now one with her coat, with the bench, the ground, and the city, she noticed the snow had melted to water on her gray suede boots. Water as clean and smooth as in Cuba. She shot up and said, almost to herself: "It's time to go home!"

THE GOLF COURSE, CHE, AND THE NUDES

I was painting almost nude. I wanted to see my torso with that damn mirror fragment poised on the easel. There was not a soul at the golf course. I know it's problematic to walk around naked in the world, but that's how it happened. What could I do?

Suddenly, Che drove up in an olive-green jeep and saw me and my uncovered torso.

I'm not afraid. I have no prejudices about my body; when drawing, a body is just one more element, stripped of lust. You feel you're in a state of grace. Che was very respectful, though I didn't stop drawing as I answered each of his questions. The jeep in the background, green on green, Che and me, forgotten by the world.

Then the full school administration appeared as if Che was on an official visit. Later came the scandal and the suggestions for an appropriate punishment, and even Celia found out.

CELIA'S REPRIMAND

Having a steaming café con leche at her home, Celia reminded me Che had a family, that it was well known even though they weren't the subject of popular magazines, she said, smiling. I listened to every word that came out of her mouth. Was she scolding me? She asked for details, argued, tried to warn me several times, frowning, but without losing her sense of humor.

She finally let me explain. I told her firmly and breathlessly how the whole thing had happened. She listened for my pauses, observed my gestures. Everything.

She opened a packet of cigarettes. She lit one Bette Davis–style and took a drag. She served me more café con leche and, more calmly, told me sometimes adults put bad ideas in young people's heads. She was sure this involved a naiveté on my part nobody could imagine, much less the school's principal. She asked me to try to understand others, that despite my obsession with painting, I couldn't just divorce myself from the real world.

She was still smoking her Chesterfields and drinking café con leche. For the first time in my presence, she let herself be carried away by her memories and spoke about her time with Che in the Sierra.

When they talked, he'd put his hand on her head or her

shoulder. When he finished, he'd walk around, then give her his notes, which she collected for her files. When he said goodbye, he'd hug her affectionately. He read a lot. Up in the mountains, he had terrible asthma attacks at two or three in the morning, so he'd step away from camp because he was very proud.

She requested different medicines to try different treatments, but the asthma never completely disappeared. Che practically devoured medical books, because he was a doctor by profession and vocation, and if someone was very sick, then he couldn't sleep a wink.

That's how she saw him.

She was sitting on the stairs, curled up with a white woven blanket, her empty mug in one hand and the Chesterfield pack in the other. Very seriously, she asked how I saw him.

"I didn't see him," I said. "His shadow fell on my face; he was backlit. I will panic, if he comes back, I'll be terrified. That's what they're going to achieve. I won't even stand to see him on TV."

What did I say! Celia found Che three days later and showed up with him at my dorm. Luckily, I was in full uniform.

From then on, whenever Che was in Cubanacán, he'd stop by the school and ask about my cohort. After that, there wasn't a day I ever let myself go uncovered. I think I got that from Celia, especially after she gave me a little blue wrap to keep myself warm. Was it some kind of hint? Maybe.

Things with Celia were resolved like that, head-on.

END OF SCHOOL—
ON THE PATH TO RADIO.
CELIA AND FIDEL AND THE
HOUSE ON ONCE STREET

She smoked Chesterfields, one after another, until her lungs couldn't take it anymore.

At the house, she brewed coffee using a cloth filter, like they do in the countryside.

Taboo subject: she was a woman alone, without children, without a husband.

She got up very late because she worked all night, just like Fidel. She didn't like to be greeted on May 9th, her birthday. She didn't like to be spoken to or flattered or recognized on the street. She tried to be inconspicuous.

She didn't sit comfortably in her chair but rather on the edge. She ate sitting on the stairs or on the couch, one leg here, the other there. And she talked the whole time. She ate very little, plate in hand. Rice, beans, salad. It was a struggle to get her to eat. She was fond of fish.

She dressed in a very special way. One day she'd don a flour sack and espadrilles, but she also wore sandals, dresses. She'd wear a suit made from sugar sacks but with a tremendous belt or a tremendous necklace and hoop earrings. She was very feminine and wore that French Rive Gauche perfume by Yves Saint Laurent. She loved to hear "Noche de ronda." At the house on Once Street, rumor had it she and Fidel loved to listen to Los Compadres.

To everyone in the house, Celia and Fidel were like one person. Relations between Celia and Fidel were casual: he'd come over and say hello, of course, and then she'd go up with him. Everyone said: "No, Celia went up to attend to him." When Fidel came over, she disappeared. She didn't get nervous or anything. Moments before his arrival, the phone would ring. As soon as he came in, she'd go up, quickly. The family always said: "When he's here, we lose Mamía."

Celia drove only little jeeps: they gave her a sports Mercedes, a BMW, an Alfa Romeo, and those two Citroën jeeps in which I always remember her. They were gifts from celebrities and heads of state linked to Cuba. The only thing they had to buy was the Fiat, because after her surgery, she couldn't handle anything else. I remember the Fiat perfectly too. There was a room full of gifts. Everything sent to her went into that room, but she barely touched those gifts; they were there in case somebody needed something. She always helped others—that was her obsession.

Her routine: She spent the early mornings at the *Granma* newspaper office, and sometimes she visited *Bohemia* magazine. She talked a lot with Carlos Franqui, the editor of *Lunes de Revolución*. She read the newspaper and reviewed letters and telegrams while having coffee in the early hours. She slept very little, but when she woke up, she would go to Lenin Park or to an office next to the Almendares River or a warehouse just off the Iron Bridge. Sometimes she had personal errands to run for Fidel, giving out gifts from the government . . . She took care of a lot of protocol projects. She didn't like having formal events at home, but she was the best when it came to prepping ceremonies for exclusive occasions. The *Atención al Pueblo* department shared her obsession of not forgetting or abandoning anyone, not leaving anyone out. The house was full of children like my sister and me, and some grew up there. She brought them from the Sierra Maestra; others left volunteer jobs and joined her on the way or wandered in. She adopted them all. Celia made us live with all that. I never understood how she managed it, but she remained discreet and at the same time transparent about everything.

In Celia's room, a landscape of the Sierra had been painted on the wall. Fidel lived upstairs, in the attic, because there was no penthouse. It was an attic, but she made it more of a loft. With a double bed. It was very modern, gabled, wood paneled, surrounded by bulletproof glass and overlooking the pool Celia had built for him. There had been nothing up there before; she had designed it all. The terrace was enclosed with wooden shutters. It was like two apartments put together. She lived in one and the other was an office. Her "private space," where she didn't allow company. She had a hammock there too, with a little light for reading. An enclosed wooden balcony. The furniture in the living room was made of cowhide, like the kind used for stools. In her bedroom there were two single beds. I've never forgotten her see-through acrylic wardrobe. She moved quickly, went in and out of it, wanted to see everything at once so as not to waste time with nonsense.

In one room she received all her good friends, but the other was much more personal. Lourdes lived downstairs with her family, then Celia, and on the top floor, Fidel, in the attic. There was a guard on the landing of each floor, always, always.

After her last trip to Japan, she couldn't smoke; she coughed a lot and didn't want to see her favorite nephew. She didn't like being seen during those coughing fits. I think Celia didn't like saying goodbye to us. Celia didn't really want to say goodbye to anyone. She wasn't weak, she wasn't easy; she was a strong woman who didn't like to expose her vulnerability.

BROADCAST FROM
THE ENEMY STATION

*Reconstruction of testimony by an unnamed person
broadcast by The Voice of the United States of America on
the day of Celia Sánchez's funeral*

Many years ago I found myself in a very difficult situation. I don't want to go into details because they're irrelevant. At that time, the tension between the US and Cuban governments was intense. I didn't sympathize with the Castro government. I stayed because I didn't want to leave; my whole family was there. Then my son developed a serious illness and the only treatment available was in the United States. He had to emigrate. When I told my family, they supported me, and I started the paperwork. But the process took a long time, and soon my son had reached military age. I despaired. There was a law—I don't know if it's still on the books—that said when a young man was summoned for military service, he couldn't leave the country. If he didn't leave immediately, his emigration could be delayed another four or five years, and his medical problem would get worse. I wrote letters to all the government agencies that might be able to deal with my case. I wrote to I don't know how many people. No one responded. No, no, that's not true. I got an answer from MINFAR, the ministry for the armed forces.

Someone (I don't know who) said they'd heard about my case but that the law was the law and they didn't have the power to change a law . . . I don't know, something like that. In other words, I was at a dead end. I didn't know where to turn, who to turn to. And then someone said, "Write to Celia." And I did. I explained my situation in detail, I listed all the steps I'd taken, the letters I'd written, my personal data—basically, everything I'd done. Although, to be frank, I didn't have much hope. I didn't believe a leader at that level would even see my letter. In the best case, a secretary might give it to someone who would take care of it, or they might say, "Look at this *gusana*,"* and file it away without doing anything about it . . .

Time passed. One day a woman came to my house asking for me and told me Celia would see me, to be at her office the next day at that same time. So I went. At the agreed time they had me go into her office. Celia was waiting for me. She got up and greeted me very warmly, with great respect, and asked how my son was doing. She invited me to sit down, and once we sat, she put her hand on a stack of open letters she had next to her on the desk.

"These are all the letters you've written," she said.

I couldn't believe it.

"It took me a little while because they had to find them all for me. But I called you because I wanted you to know your case has been heard. And we'll see what we can do to resolve it. Don't worry. We'll find a solution."

* *gusana/o*—literally, "worm"; derogatory term used to describe those opposed to the Castro government.

So it was. I don't know how, but the truth is that sometime later my son and I were on a plane, legally, with all the papers arranged so we could go to the United States. I never wrote to thank her. I don't know if it was because I thought she'd be offended—after all, I was a malcontent—or maybe because her very attitude had seemed to say, "You don't need to thank me." I don't know. When you need so much because you're helpless and suddenly someone comes and helps you just because, out of a sense of humanity . . . Sometimes I've thought that if I'd written a letter to thank her for what she'd done for me, she wouldn't have paid much attention to it.

CASTRO AND FLYNN

In an article written by Errol Flynn in February 1959, everyone is gathered in a small room. People are coming and going. There is a revolver lying on the table, as well as one glued to the tiny waist of Celia Sánchez. Flynn pins her measurements at 36-24-35. Castro is Flynn's height more or less. He has a smooth face, a relaxed demeanor, and a fine handshake. Celia fixes his glasses for him without hesitation. Through an interpreter, they become fond—Castro becomes Fidel and Flynn becomes Errol.

Flynn writes with a Hollywood eye. The big picture is only interesting to him if he is starring in it.

NOTES
(FIDEL: DETAILS, HABITS, STYLE)

From the notes that José Pardo Llada wrote about the early days and time in the Sierra, we know, among other things, that Fidel smoked constantly. That he spoke softly and had an exceptional memory. That his beard-stroking was his trademark tic and that he was slightly myopic and rotated between six pairs of eyeglasses. He wore two watches on his left wrist. And, in Celia's recollection, he was an expert in breaking both glasses and wristwatches. He read when he could: *The Memoirs of Marshal Mannerheim, The Power Elite, The Complete Works of José Martí.* Also, a book about ranching. He wrote quickly in small, neat, handwriting. Celia copied the most important documents. He had three photos in his cabin at Providencia, all of them of his son.

THE LAST TIME I SAW HER

One day I saw Celia crying at her desk. She wasn't a woman inclined to cry, so maybe it was just my imagination. Another time I knocked on her bedroom door again and again, and she didn't respond. I left without talking to her.

We hadn't spoken for a long time. But that day I wanted to say hi to her. We were conducting interviews in what would later become Lenin Park when I saw her working off to the side, in a secluded little place.

I left the group. The people from the station hadn't realized Celia's car was right there. She didn't have the jeep anymore, and she was driving a new Fiat. I went in, through an area where they were laying marble, and I sat down to wait for her to come by. She had a habit of going to the car to get cigarettes and a wrap.

Finally, she was right in front of me. Smoking like a chimney. With her thin, veiny hands, her black hair tied with a bow, and a wildflower pinned to her ear. She went to hug me. She tried to say she was okay, but I knew she wasn't. She looked exhausted. Dark circles under her eyes, the shakes. She was no longer the woman I'd met when I'd first come to Havana. I sat down with her, and we started talking something like this, while she lit one Chesterfield after another:

CELIA: Pucha told me your sister left the country.

ME: I tried to see you to tell you what happened.

CELIA: Why did she leave? I thought she wanted to finish her degree and become a specialist.

ME: She was working long hours at the morgue because she said it was too hot in the guesthouse. She was tired, and my parents asked her to join them. My sister was going crazy, Celia. She only talked about tumors, instruments for cutting cadavers; she was all alone with her microscope. It was time, and now she's gone. I feel guilty she stayed to take care of me; no one can take care of me.

CELIA: It's a shame. But even my own family members have left because of this or that. We need to be present here and now.

ME: I can't take it anymore. I'm next.

CELIA: I don't think so. You're here because you can be.

ME: Since I was expelled from the ENA because of that incident, I can't stand or approve of questioning people's intimate lives; it's outrageous. No family can survive that. There's no respect, I don't want my daughter—

CELIA: How is your daughter?

ME: The girl's perfect. Children are very strong, and they encourage you to go on in the midst of everything you can't deal with by yourself. We've been through a lot. I can't stand it when they get in my life, violate our privacy, or question me.

CELIA: Do you know what they say about me? Even if you know, you're not going to tell me. But I know what they say about me.

Celia stared at me, with her piercing black eyes. She coughed, smoked, breathed heavily.

ME: The people love you very much. You know that.

CELIA: I'm not stupid. They love me because I'm with them all the time, I see them, I touch them, I'm on the streets every day. But for that very reason, because I'm here, I know there are others who don't like me much. Things aren't black and white. They say I'm a witch, or that, because I protect homosexuals, I might be one too. I've never married and that provides fuel for the fire. This is like in Manzanillo, the old women who remained single like me—there was always a story about them. They talk and I play dumb. They say I'm married to . . . Well, my nieces are my daughters. So many things have been said about me! They even said I supported the executions. But the only person you have to please is yourself. You can't live waiting to see what the rumors are. You have to have your own integrity and not be led by what others say. Ah, but if you leave because of what they say, then you're not who I think you are. Forgive me.

Celia wanted to leave and walked out to her car. She asked me to go with her. On the way, for a moment, as if we were thinking about it at the same time, we both said my sister's name, and I suddenly missed her a lot. Not the crazy pathologist but the straight-forward sister who stared at Celia on the way out of the Habana Libre, back in the days when we'd just arrived in the capital as literacy teachers.

CELIA: Why do people leave us like that, huh?

ME: It's not because of a rumor, you can be sure of that.

CELIA: The other day I had some tests done. I was talking to a pathologist. I thought so much about your sister. She would have told me the truth. She didn't mince words. She reminds me of Griseda, my sister—she's like her, unstoppable. She has a great sense of humor.

We laughed and then we were silent until we reached the city, the only sounds her coughing and the windshield wipers. It was drizzling very lightly, and once again, Havana looked like a miniature model before us. Whenever I was with Celia, I felt as if the city could change, modify, move, improve. And I saw everything quietly, from above.

ME: Celia, you never liked the idea of being First Lady?
CELIA: You say such crazy things! When, my friend? I was never the First Lady. That's not for me. I've never thought about anything so sublime; there's too much to do down here. You can't deny you studied at a Protestant American college. Get out of the car. We're here.

I stayed at the Once Street house until dawn. She wouldn't stop coughing; she could barely breathe. We called her doctor. Waiting for him, we talked about others who'd left. She didn't have the strength to argue anymore, but she argued anyway. She had a bad cough and wouldn't stop smoking. If I stayed a few more years, it was only because of my daughter and because of Celia. Because I didn't want to upset them, although Celia and I never saw each other again. That was the last night.

IDEAS/NOTES

Celia's fundamental nature: an absolute abandonment of individual interests in service of others.

Her attitude: a conscious vocation of surrender. Service as a natural duty that doesn't require recognition or encouragement.

How it manifests: going unnoticed.

The conflict: the Revolution as a way of life, and once in, you can't get out. Stopping equals death. You can only go forward. But that struggle claims lives. Each step demands its share of blood.

Her pain: Celia was part of a group of wholesome young people, educated for noble causes, who voluntarily assumed the possibility of martyrdom: Abel, Renato, Juan Manuel, Alomá, Tey, Frank and Josué, José Antonio, Lidia, Clodomira, Ramos Latour, Ángel, Gustavo and Machaco Ameijeiras, El Vaquerito, Paco Cabrera, Camilo, Che, San Luis, and many others. There were also those she recruited or she knew from Manzanillo who signed up: Ignacio Pérez, Beto Pesant, Braulio Coroneaux, Ciro Frías, René Vallejo, Piti Fajardo.

Of all those young people who sparked the Revolution and participated in all the battles, only four survived: Fidel and Raúl Castro, Juan Almeida, and Ramiro Valdés.

Haydée Santamaría was overwhelmed by so many deaths

and took her own life. The difference between her and Celia is that, in the long run, Celia could have overcome all possible deaths, except one.

Her religion: We don't know if she kept her faith in the Sierra thanks to Father Guillermo Sardiñas, chaplain of the Rebel Army. With the triumph of the Revolution, she underwent a drastic change. According to her, when the clergy announced that churches would be used as a political platform against the Revolution, many Catholics abandoned their religion. Celia chose to stop attending mass because, being a figure so high up in the political hierarchy, her presence in the pews would have been controversial.

Her daily routine: sticking to the three basic principles of guerrilla life as articulated by Che—constant vigilance, constant movement, constant action—and working at night, sleeping infrequently, discarding the superfluous, eating only to fulfill biological needs, dressing quickly, valuing personal items only for their utility, and being self-sufficient.

Her magic: she had no military rank or relevant positions, yet she embodied the noble aspects of the Revolution.

There is talk of a possible love affair between Fidel Castro and Celia Sánchez. There's no real evidence, and nobody wants to dig any deeper into it. If it's true, it's such a secret that anything that might be said about it would be fanciful, not serious. And it's not relevant. To make Fidel and Celia a couple would be to vulgarize the story.

When Fidel was in Mexico organizing the guerrillas, Celia hadn't met him yet, but she'd already carried out an enormous amount of work, recruiting a vast network of collaborators to support the landing of the yacht, the *Granma*, which transported rebels exiled in Mexico back to Cuba. And when this finally happened, under the most adverse conditions imaginable, she committed herself to sending reinforcements and the means of subsistence to the decimated guerrilla group, thereby guaranteeing their survival.

Celia met Fidel in person in February 1957—that is, almost four years after the attack on the Moncada barracks. After this meeting, did her devotion to Fidel increase to an unthinkable degree? Yes. But she wasn't the only one. Fidel enthralled both men and women. The difference was that, being a woman, she was closer to him than anyone else and had the power to do what no one else would have been allowed to do.

And for these reasons, after the Revolution triumphed, Celia—without military rank or an important position in the government—became the female figure with the highest moral and political position in the country. No one questioned it; she was surpassed only by Fidel and Raúl Castro. That's how it was until her death.

HOW FIDEL FOUND OUT
BATISTA HAD FLED

New Year's Eve, 1958, Camp Columbia. The General Army of the Rebel Command arrived at the camp after having stayed late in Palma Soriano. Rumors were circulating that Batista's family fled. Fidel kept pacing restlessly on the porch. At eight in the morning came a TV newsflash from Radio Progreso. They reported that journalists are currently waiting for updates on the situation at Camp Columbia . . .

Fidel shot to his feet. Indignant, he rushed to the dining room door and then turned around.

Fidel ordered, "We can no longer wait. We must attack Santiago as soon as possible. If they are so naive that they believe they'll stop the Revolution with a coup, we're going to show them how wrong they are."

Luis, who was in charge of the ammunition and other war materials (as well as the Commander's dental hygiene) asked for fifteen more minutes.

People came and went, offering new bits of information.

The radio announced that Cantillo had taken over army headquarters. The new president was Piedra, a Supreme Court magistrate. Batista fled to Santo Domingo.

In the midst of all the hubbub, according to José Pardo

Llada, Fidel leaned against an armoire and took out a notebook—the kind that sell for five cents at Woolworth's.

Ten minutes later, he read his instructions to all Rebel Army comandantes and the people.

INSTRUCTIONS FROM THE GENERAL COMMAND TO ALL THE COMANDANTES OF THE REBEL ARMY AND THE PEOPLE

NO MATTER the news from the capital, our forces must continue their operations against the enemy on all fronts.

Agree to talks only with garrisons that wish to surrender.

Apparently, there's been a coup in the capital. The Rebel Army is unaware of the conditions in which that coup has taken place.

The people must be very alert and heed only the instructions of the General Command. The dictatorship has collapsed as a result of the crushing defeats suffered in the last weeks.

HOW WE GOT THE NEWS (I)

That Tuesday I was filling the tub. I hopped in, thinking there might be enough water. It was better to take advantage of it and use what I could. Days when we had water: Monday, Wednesday, and Friday.

If the schedule was altered, then towns fell behind, ended up owing one another, and we could go five days without water. This is a country where practical things are not in the service of the people, and so we live focused on practicalities. It's incredible. We might dedicate a whole day to the water problem. Opening the faucet and letting water run isn't a fact of life in Cuba.

I was with my daughter in bed. There was nothing to do; I was in a daze, rereading my radio scripts, smoking.

Everybody steals my ideas. My programs on the old *soneros* are taken out of the country and become collectors' items, even when they're only annotations, sound logs. That's what I was thinking when I grabbed the bucket and went to deal with the water.

The veins on my hands have popped out from raising and lowering the damned buckets of water. I've picked so much coffee in my life and today there was nothing for my coffee pot, neither water nor coffee. It was awful! An empty stomach nauseates me. I go up and down, up and down

328 steps to fill a tub built in 1936. I was half finished when Pucha showed up, crying, and sat on the lacquered end of the bathtub.

"You see? This is over. I knew she was dying. They told me she wasn't, but look," she said.

I turned on the radio, but they hadn't said anything yet. Nothing at all.

I tried to wake Nadia so we could go with Pucha. The girl was exhausted, and we let her have five more minutes in bed.

I got into the tub full of water and lathered myself. Scrubbed my skin hard with good shampoo and soap. I rinsed, contaminating the clean water. The next five waterless days didn't matter anymore. "Now it's started," I told myself. I was thinking of Celia's dead face, her eyes closed. Butterflies around her, people crying. Everything that would come hit me like a flash. It was wild, but I saw her floating like Ophelia on the water, butterflies hovering above the surface, the same butterflies Raúl Martínez had painted for her. The foam kept me from seeing the gnawed bottom of what once had been white; nothing was white anymore. There was an orange mist all around my feet. Something was rusting down there. Nothing would ever be the same again. Pucha's face said it all. Tears, rust, and soap.

Part IV

I WAS NEVER THE FIRST LADY

DIRT OR BLOOD?

Heartbroken, I finish reading what the customs agents left of my mother's papers.

Now I'll be the one to research Celia. I'm going to write my mother's novel, though I know that today, in Cuba, it's going to be hard for me. Even if I get through everything in her inaccessible office, I won't know much more. There are stop signs, traffic lights, in there. Everything has been sealed. That office is about others; she took her body and soul elsewhere. What they treasure no longer contains her.

We think we know everything about the lives of others. We think we know everything about our own lives, but it's not true. They keep us vigilant, trained for life as part of the herd. Hunting other people's gestures and symptoms. We explain without being asked. Not being exposed is suspicious in a society where surveillance is entrenched even in urban planning. We believe we know everything about others and, furthermore, that we know every aspect of ourselves, perhaps because here the light leaves no possibility of mystery, but that's not true. When we get close to the lives of others, the ignorance of our own universe is exacerbated. It's fascinating: you lose yourself and begin to embody the character you're tracking. Celia has sealed her shelves, closed the fire exits; her secrets have been burned forever.

Her work was dedicated to the preservation of others' stories. She kept every piece of paper, wrote down what was important, even if no one else could see it in the moment. She was absolutely transparent. She was sure any trace of her would disrupt the existence of others, that any infringement would spoil her intention. Her footprints linger in their history. In that, she's like my mother, who preserved what seemed lost then and today can only be re-created by others.

CELIA'S WAKE, MY MOTHER, BUTTERFLIES, THE PEOPLE

I remember almost all the parades I went to. I also remember my mother keeping quiet so she could skip certain parades. She had complicated reasons for not going, and every time she explained them to me she would cry, and then I would stop understanding what she was trying to tell me; I'd just obey. I would swallow hard because I couldn't stand to see her cry, especially over a simple parade my friends were going to with their mothers. We always went to the same parade. It was just one parade, but it was very loooong.

I can't find anything about Celia's funeral in the black cardboard box, nothing about when my mother took me to see her and we left a flower for her. We spent hours in line on Paseo Street. Finally, we entered a large room with marble floors, a flag, and many flowers. I didn't see the body; I kept my eyes closed. My mother picked me up so I could blow her a kiss. I kept my eyes squeezed shut and blew.

I was scared; I don't know what I might have actually seen, and I decided to forget the images. My mother said she was a friend. To me she was a dead body.

I hate the smell of Butterflies (a Cuban cologne) because it makes me go back to the scene with my mother's dead friend, to her sadness. I thought she would die from crying so much.

I've never gone to a parade again. Parades are where my country celebrates its great events, but I always relate them to my mother's pain. Seeing the Plaza de la Revolución and sensing the smell of Butterflies is the same for me.

I see people crying as I walk by, my mother crying . . . I lose myself in the sea of tears, I stop being me and turn into my mother, tears scattered on the ground, tears that drown me in nostalgia. It's a decision: I don't go to places where death rips me apart.

THE DUST-JACKETED
LIBRARY

My childhood home was partitioned—the space I shared with my mother measured less than forty square meters—but in spite of this, we had two libraries. I was little when Mami left, but I still remember the two libraries.

One could be viewed easily, with a front row of shelves jammed with biographies, diaries, novels, poetry books, and behind it, camouflaged, a library with books in homemade dust jackets in a secret space, our friends' favorite labyrinth.

When someone spoke in the past tense about someone else who'd once visited and had coffee in our living room, it was because that someone was no longer with us. When this person was quoted in a low voice, with nicknames or surnames that became unspeakable, when the only copy of a book was opened before the eyes of another friend, it was because that book came with a homemade dust jacket. It was a book "illuminated by hand." Renamed with harmless titles like: *Crafts. College of Friends. How to Learn Without Suffering* by J. J. Almirall.

These books ended up in the back, in the deep darkness, disappeared into an invisible architecture, into the labyrinth where the most desired readings rested. These were damp books that served us like the tools of the Count of Monte

Cristo. Each one arrived at my house via a different means. These were "the rough years," and so we had to hide rough texts.

This list of titles wasn't shared with everyone, nor were the books loaned to just anyone; they actually never left the house. They were read standing up between improvised meals and coffee made from recycled grounds.

My mother was always the veiled queen of this small circle of apprentices. She enjoyed and suffered from the halo conferred on her because she couldn't—she wasn't able to (or didn't want to)—publish her poetry. In the 1970s, she submitted an original manuscript to one of Cuba's few publishing houses, but they never responded. That's as far as her efforts went. It wasn't just censorship. My mother couldn't have published anywhere. She was a brilliant long-distance thinker. She brought together a group of artists who are now part of the Cuban intelligentsia active inside and outside Cuba. My house was a meeting place for many poets, the axis of debates, headaches, parties, arguments, tears, goodbyes, and disappointments for those who weren't accepted as part of the diversity of opinions at that time.

If a friend fell from grace, my mother would rescue them. She catalogued books to protect them; this way the volumes with the homemade dust jackets eventually reached more than three hundred readers. And since the end of many of those friendships almost always came about because the friends emigrated, we kept the books safe.

When I finally read them, my mother wasn't with me anymore. She'd fired everyone and left without saying goodbye to anyone. Little by little she'd been trying to answer these questions: What could justify censorship—a book's author or its contents? Can certain authors and titles be eliminated in Cuba for an entire lifetime?

My mother's "nest" has been resettled; the same dark place now hides her treasure box. She pulls seven carefully covered books from her purse and continues to ponder matters of trust. It's fear that confuses her and makes everything difficult.

When I met Eliseo Diego, I was eight years old, and I asked my mother: "Mami, does he write 'covered' books?"

"No, he writes poems to recite from memory," she said, "but he belongs to the generation of 'covered' books." (His son, Eliseo Alberto Diego, "Lichi," was an heir to the Orígenes group, and he wrote "covered" books too.)

Right now, we're stripping the books of their homemade dust jackets.

I bring my mother out to the porch. I cover her because the sea air is treacherous. I help her settle in the wooden rocking chair she's taken over these days. I want her to see our ritual from a front-row seat. Our requests, our prayers, are fulfilled at last.

Lujo and I light a pyre in the garden overlooking the Malecón. Then we take the coverings, the gags, the masks, the chastity belts, from the books, peeling off their fears, throwing aside the jackets so the fire can devour them. Some jackets have pictures of martyrs; others, the faces of Russian models; the most recent, ads and posters for American movies.

The fire makes us delirious. My mother doesn't quite know why, but she claps when she sees the flames.

Lujo cries and I laugh. I don't want to forget this moment. This is freedom by fire, my little historical revenge. The time has come to open these treasures, to reveal what they are and let them go out into the dense air of the Havana Malecón. A golden light illuminates the names and surnames.

Dear authors: I give you Havana in full color.

I wonder when they'll be allowed through customs, or when they're going to be published in Cuba once and for all. Not one more hidden book, not one more silenced word. That is my greatest wish as a citizen.

My library is empty, and now I have to save my mother. Before she completely loses her memory, let me unveil the original covers. I give her the pleasure of seeing them in all their splendor, even if she doesn't understand anything, even if it's too late for her. How wonderful to look at them together before they go into the fire! I read exile classics just like I read the classics still here but dying.

No question about it. A good book is meant to be published for its natural audience, in its homeland, with the taste of its origins, the smell and feel of how it was originally intended. Books are meant to be read. Run your finger over their bare covers and choose the command for those of us who want to listen and be heard freely.

Down with homemade dust jackets!

My mother claps. Lujo keeps crying. I take photos to capture the moment. My new artwork.

MONOLOGUE WITH THE TV

There's an interview with Fidel, maybe by an Argentine journalist on TV. It was not conducted in Cuba. I try, a little late, to write down the things Mami is saying in response to Fidel from her chair.

FIDEL: Yes, it seemed like a triumph of the Revolution, but everything still had to be organized.

MAMI: We were all with you. I swear by my daughter, Nadia, whom I haven't seen in twenty years.

JOURNALIST: The overthrow of that regime brought on a new government led by people who were quite inexperienced.

FIDEL: So what? Tell me, so what? Find me a better model, and I swear to you I'd do my best; I'd start fighting all over again for another fifty years for that new model.

MAMI: That model should be about opening up to the world. I told you they were cheating you. That no one can come to or leave Cuba if they don't have permission. I told you this was going to drive you crazy, because people need to feel they can come and go, even if they have nowhere to go or the means to pay for it. Oh, Fidel! This is the way it is, but you have to travel and see a bit of the world without so many bodyguards, my friend.

JOURNALIST: How do you imagine the future of Cuba, when Castro isn't center stage?

FIDEL: Many people ask that question. I ask myself too.

MAMI: You have to leave with everything taken care of, because if you don't, who knows who will crawl through the window, and the Americans, who only want to screw Cuba, will soon be here again. Hurry, my friend, you're not a young man anymore. Hurry up. I've been warning you for twenty years, and you're still infatuated, like a little boy with an ice cream cone you won't share that just melts in your hand. Hurry up, Fidel. We're with you.

JOURNALIST: So then?

FIDEL: The mistake is to believe Castro is everything, because you say: Castro does this . . . Castro does that. For example, I can give myself credit, though I'm a little embarrassed—I mean, I don't want to exalt personal things, far from it. Let's look at the idea of how to solve the Batista problem when the coup took place on March 10th. We didn't have a penny or any weapons, and there was a tremendous force confronting us. Moreover, nobody was paying much attention to us because the overthrown government had resources and the support of many army officers. We decided that, despite everything, the problem could be dealt with. But there's not much merit when luck plays such an oversized role. Because you can ask me: "Why are you here?" And I'll say it's a question of chance, among other things. But there are ideas. This problem was very difficult, and there were also great personal risks, but it could be solved.

MAMI: Listen to what I'm going to tell you. You're everything because you and I know we wanted it that way. But now we have to pass the baton to the young, because you're not

eternal. I'm going to have a fit because you're not listening
to me. You don't listen to me . . . Girl, girl, turn off the TV
because I'm going to have a breakdown—and don't turn
it on again until Fidel calls me. Until he comes to tell me
what's new, don't turn it on! He's being deceived. Deceived.
No one has the nerve to tell him what he needs to hear. If
Celia were alive, she would've told him clearly. If he didn't
lose touch with reality and the people before, it was because
she kept him current on everything. Without deifying him.
She talked truth to power.

"Mami, calm down."

"Turn off that thing and bring me the radio; he doesn't talk
like that on the radio."

I turn off the TV and realize she is crying very quietly into
one of Lujo's handkerchiefs. I turn on the National Radio
newscast for her. I stay with her for a while. I run my hand
through her hair.

"Mami, who am I?"

"My sister."

"And your daughter?"

"In Havana."

"And where are you now?"

"In limbo. Let me cry in peace for a while, by myself, to
see if I can forget this too."

She falls asleep on the rocking chair. When Lujo comes
home, it is after nine o'clock. I read the notes I took of what
she said because I don't want to forget. Lujo begins to cry too.

"If they loved this so much, how could they walk away
and leave us alone?" I ask.

"You'll understand eventually, Nadia. For you, it starts

now. Your mom once spoke to Fidel at the house on Once Street. But no one knows what they talked about because she wasn't one to divulge that kind of thing. Apparently it was something interesting, because she left energized enough to want to take on the world. They assigned her to the station, and that's where her life in radio began. That's why it took her so long to leave, after art school . . . Things changed a lot after Celia died. People no longer ran into Fidel on the street, like before."

"Do you know what they talked about, or don't you want to tell me?"

"That conversation was in the stolen novel. If you didn't find anything among the documents in the box, forget it. She never told anyone. Maybe it's still in that lost head of hers. Nadia, at this point it's better not to know anything about the past. Live now—this is your moment. I'm going to bed. I'm taking your mother to bed. Turn off the radio."

PAIN AND FORGIVENESS

I went to the hotel, and the guard asked, like they always did, where I was going.

"I'm going to meet a friend."

The guard replied, "A friend?"

Luckily, Paolo B. was already at the hotel door. It's the site of so many sins, secrets, clean and dirty businesses.

"This hotel is suspicious of me."

Paolo hugged me and decided to kiss me on the forehead. We went down to the restaurant by the pool. We sat facing each other. Paolo was different without a coat, unshaven. He'd taken off his helmet and shield and had come unarmed. Now he was indeed Cuban; he spoke like us, gestured like us, touched my skin, widened his eyes, made faces as he talked. What a transformation.

"Three words: you're my daughter. These are the papers. You're my daughter. We can't see each other any other way."

I looked at him uncertainly. My father's face was coming into my head—I couldn't help it. I reviewed the papers, clipped together, along with other documents from an Italian court. I don't understand Italian. I could think only of the sequence of our lovemaking. I surrendered to Paolo, but there was no use crying here, since the collapse was entirely mine, and no one else needed to take part in my disaster—another disaster; it seems I can handle more after all. The papers lay in front of me.

We were waiting for something.

"What do I have to do?"

"Sign below. What's mine is yours, what's yours is mine. I don't have any children—that is, I have no other children."

I signed the papers without pause, not looking at him. He tried to make a sort of speech, but I wasn't listening. He talked about compensation as if money were the answer. I don't know what he could compensate me for. This mess was coming from somewhere else. A parade of past grudges resolved themselves.

I decided to look at him. I hadn't heard his voice in a long time. I tried to see his features in mine. He said his family was from Pinar del Río, that his father owned tobacco fields, that he looked a lot like his mother . . . Now a new grandmother, now a new house . . .

"What nonsense, Nadia! How did I not realize you're just like my mother?"

I took a deep breath. If I paid attention, I'd start to vomit.

A tour guide went by talking like an automaton, telling the story of the Hotel Nacional. While Paolo B. was experiencing a catharsis in front of me, I had closed off. It was as if I'd just turned off the sound and muted Paolo.

Tourist guide: "Located on the coastal overhang of Punta Brava, on the Taganana hill almost at the end of the San Lázaro cove, this was a common site for pirate landings. Cuba's Hotel Nacional has stood here since December 30th, 1930, the most important hotel in the Greater Caribbean. This hill we're on was the famous Santa Clara sugar plantation in the mid-nineteenth century. The Ordóñez cannon, one of the biggest of its time, is still in the hotel gardens. Near Punta Brava, the councilman Don Luis Aguiar overcame the British during their siege and assault on Havana . . ."

It was pathetic to see him cry over me, the girl, over me, the lover. It seemed ridiculous to me that this man should be my father and that I'd put on that gymnastics sex show in his living room, far from this tangible, crude, Cuban reality of mine.

I was mired in the disaster, and worst of all, I knew I'd never recover from it. The past tugged on my hair, yanked me out of myself. I stopped listening to Paolo again and observed the visitors and mobsters in the hotel.

Tourist guide: "Among its first illustrious visitors were celebrities from the worlds of art and literature, such as Johnny Weissmuller, Buster Keaton, José Mojica, Jorge Negrete, Agustín Lara, Tyrone Power, Rómulo Gallegos, Errol Flynn, Marlon Brando, and the famous Ernest Hemingway, who donated a stuffed blue marlin for our bar, Sirena . . ."

I don't want any more information about the past. The past seems to bring only bad news. The present is my business. The past is stuck on these hippies and urban guerrillas who made love to each other as an offensive against those of us who came later. I kissed Paolo B. on the cheek and left the room. In my new role as a grown-up orphan, I couldn't bear to hear him anymore. He asked for forgiveness, please. This seemed like a song by Benny Moré.

> Sorry, sorry, sweet darling,
> sorry for abandoning you.

I was thinking of everything I wanted to say, but I didn't have the strength to attend to my mother, sing truths to Paolo, overcome the death of my father, and accept Paolo and his family in Pinar del Río, never mind doing my work. I chose my battles. I had to swallow that bitter pill. It was the end—no more bad news. I'd hit rock bottom. Paolo had taken ownership of some land in Pinar del Río, something related to the expropriation of some farmland. He wanted me to find out about this, now that I was his daughter. I took a deep breath.

"Don't be ridiculous. It's not time. Let me try to understand."

I ran across the garden. Paolo quickened his pace to catch up with me. Everything was bad except Havana. The beauty of the oceanfront garden seemed to contradict me. The sea surrounds us, saves and drowns us. It's what makes us sleep with the same people, dream about them, give birth to them, hate them . . . and love them, despite the sea and despite them. I wanted to say to him: "You people are never going to pay for what you did to us. You're so irresponsible." We hugged at the hotel door. I didn't say anything. I remembered I'd offered to make love to him in Paris, using the same seduction my mother had when they were lovers.

"I forgive you because I forgive myself, but don't talk about the past anymore. I'm here and that's enough. That's enough."

Paolo asked if he could see my mother, that he'd come for four days and still had to visit Pinar del Río. I told him tomorrow, with friends, at lunchtime. Today wasn't a good day anymore.

As I left the hotel, the guard smirked. "A friend, eh? What kind of little friend is that?"

There were no answers, there aren't always answers, no coherent responses to the simplest things. I went down the little hill on the Hotel Nacional grounds and crossed the tennis courts as the security guards tipped each other off when I passed. I skirted the fenced pool. I heard guests splashing about in their socialist tropics.

I reached the street at the violet hour, my body and my gray dress colored a purplish blue. There wasn't much left of the afternoon, just a moment. I crossed to the Malecón and wondered why they don't sell pizzas at La Piragua, why they don't fix the little houses eaten away by salt. Why? Why? Why this sea of flags if no one can save us? Has anyone seen us? Does anyone see us?

NOTE

No one home. I tremble with fear. I keep writing in my diary.

PURE THEATER

"ello, Nadia, little Nadia. Anybody here?"

"You scared me. I didn't see anyone and I thought . . . Mami can't be left alone. I just got here. I have to tell you something. It's very—"

"You're crying?" Lujo asked. "Your mother wasn't lost. Stop being so melodramatic. Look how beautiful I've dressed her to go out. They're your clothes, but not really. What's wrong? You don't like it? You can tell me your story later—mine first. I went out with your mother. We went to the theater. The Amadeo Roldán is very nicely restored; I have so many memories of that auditorium. Not this one (*pointing at Mami*), because she doesn't even remember how to sit down anymore. (She's happier this way, overall, given what she has to remember.) We went to see Gidon Kremer and his Kremerata Baltica. It was a spectacular concert. I felt such nostalgia for the Soviets, especially for those chubby Baltic women, who dress so much better now, with bouquets in their hands. They played pieces by Cherubini, something rabidly contemporary. (I thought of you, trying to conjure you, but you postmodernists have more cultural gaps than us, the elders.) They also played something by Kancheli, Shostakovich, and closed with the 'Suite Punta del Este' by Piazzolla. The encore was by Piazzolla too and then something from the soundtrack of a spaghetti western—I think it was *A Fist-ful of Dollars*. They had fun, the musicians. They were having a great time—you could tell. The public behaved like never before; I didn't have to scold anyone for talking. We were hypnotized. The only sour note was the chlorine, or rather the lack of chlorine. The restrooms in the Amadeo stink like a zoo in summer. What would Roldán say?"

"I'm glad you took Mami with you."

"Let me finish the story before you tell me your problem. We started clapping and yelling, 'Bravo! Viva!' There was a standing ovation, people threw flowers, you know, all that stuff we do here to honor our guests. In the midst of the euphoria there was a brief silence, and suddenly your mother shouts, 'Long live Fidel!' I can't describe the effect that had: it stunned the room into complete silence. We ran out of there. Horrors! What a terrible misunderstanding! This poor woman. She can only communicate with the TV now."

"I can't bear one more problem, Lujo. Paolo B. is here. I've just come from his hotel. Things are worse than I thought."

"Paolo B. is here? Mmmmm. What happened to his peasant fear of planes?"

"He told me you knew everything . . ."

"No one knows less than me. I don't have a radio, I don't read the papers, and I disconnected the antenna in my room since we moved here. I don't watch TV, even in the living room. My neurons are taking a break, and I avoid getting upset and having one-way arguments with the mus-tachioed man on the news. And in any case, what's done is done."

"What's done is done because of my parents and all of you—I'm the result of this dysfunctional family."

"God forbid we should start using such pedagogical terms in this house . . ."

"I'm going to put Mami to bed, and then you and I can talk . . ."

I tuck my mother in like a child every night. I sing to her. I read something she likes so she won't forget my voice. I know all is lost, that she came here to die, that she thinks I'm her sister.

I turn off the light when she falls asleep. I go out to the living room and write in my diary until I can't anymore.

The house is dark, and the amber glass lamps flicker until dawn. The Malecón ruminates on its fears, and frightened, I check on my mother two or three times a night, just to make sure she's breathing.

I'll have to watch her die. I won't be able to avoid it. This is us: my mother at last, me taking care of her. The roles have been reversed, but it's time to admit it: I'm not an ordinary woman; I never will be.

I don't know whether to argue with Lujo. He's the only person who sustains me, who feeds me and makes my life better. Lujo is my stepmother.

My mother never said who my real father was. Did she know? Why was she expelled from art school? Was she in love with my father or with Paolo? There are so many unanswered questions! The worst part is that I don't need answers anymore. Those libertine lives at camps, with *trova* music as a soundtrack, those were the hallmark of the '60s and '70s. I'm the saga. I made advances like an untrained animal on one of my mother's lovers. What did she do to compel me to look for him? Was it a ridiculous calling of blood or a simple list of names? I hate lists. Trembling crowds. Groups, collective affiliations. Like in mathematics, we're facing a problem with no solution.

It's real life, and I'm putting an end to this long break, to our sunny summer. I sweep away this hangover, launder the dirty linens of her irresponsibility. I throw away my mother's soiled diapers and wash her clean. I teach her to eat when she forgets.

THE LIVING WAKE

They all arrive as I am cutting the corn from the cob. The sofrito, with pork and shrimp, is ready, but I still need to stir and wait for the sauce to set. My friend Dania was passing through Havana. Since she'd graduated from the School of Letters, she hadn't wanted to know about the city until today, when she came from Cienfuegos to defend her doctoral thesis. Now she's obsessed with aesthetics and only talks about meta this and meta that. Definitions and concepts that hurt and confuse. Anyhow, I love her the way she is. Her home is far away, and we can never talk other than on the phone. It's a known fact: you create something and critics dismember it, dissecting the soul of things. They turn artists into hospital patients, especially if we're talking bodies in performances, like mine. Dania loves me, but she's my worst critic. She's the only childhood friend I have left in Cuba. I have to take care of her like an heirloom.

For Dania, my mother's a mystery. She can't believe she's still alive. She'd always expected that, on one of our collective birthdays at school, my mother would show up with a huge doll and sing together with the other classroom parents: "*Felicidad, felicidad, felicidad*, ehhhhh!"

Poor Dania—life was so simple for her. If she sees aesthetics that way, we're all lost.

I leave Dania on the computer reading Diego's letters. After all the time we've spent together, there can be no secrets. Dania loses herself in the liquid crystal of the screen.

Old friends are talking at the round table. I cook for them. Mami stares blankly. They all speak carefully, as if she were foreign or deaf.

The dialogue is stilted. I thought we'd get together and it would be like the old days, as if no time had passed, but no. Time passes, unforgivingly.

They drink, chatter, raise their voices, laugh, cry. Little by little they warm up, but I notice something. They can't bring back their former selves. They can't catch the rhythm of being among trusted friends. I'm the observer, the cook, the host; I'm the daughter.

PAOLO B.: It's not enough to survive—you have to live every minute.

ADRIANA: Given the number of people who have died at our age, fuck politics and fuck the past. To life.

They toast with a fruity French wine Paolo B. brought for the occasion.

PAOLO B.: To this reunion, and to our health, which is the most important thing.

He says this smiling like a provincial undertaker while looking right at Mami.

MAMI: Health comes and goes—just look at me. The important thing is money.

The friends make an effort not to laugh, but it's impossible.

PAOLO B.: See what politics does!

He says this once more nodding toward my mother.

LUJO: Politics is like salt—we wouldn't be able to cook our daily meals without it. We wouldn't be able to take sides and support this or that candidate, or take a position . . .

ADRIANA: Lujo, that's you, who went for a walk and came back twenty years later; there's no salt here. Politics is only one way here, and not very entertaining, I must say.

ALINA: Oh, guys, why don't we stop talking about *him*? I came here to talk about *her*.

She says this looking at my mother.

MAMI: Good evening. Are we going to listen to my show now? Can I get a radio, please?

NADIA: We're here to share a meal. The program's over.

MAMI: I told you to let me know. I don't know anyone.

NADIA: Look, I'll introduce you to them one by one.

MAMI: No, no, they're crazy and talk about things I don't understand. Don't count on me to make friends with them; they're conspirators.

ALINA: Oh, I can't handle this (*cries*). Don't you remember me, your best friend? How could this happen to you?

MAMI, *making a dismissive gesture while staring at Alina*: I told you no, to leave me alone.

PAOLO B.: It's politics that did this to her. This system drove her insane.

ADRIANA: But she's spent half her life out of the country.

PAOLO B.: Running away, running away from the system. It drove her crazy.

ALINA: Nadia, my dear . . . how was it for you to see her come back like this?

NADIA: She's here. It's a relief.

ADRIANA: But, look, we're not all like this; that's a false notion of what we've experienced.

JOSÉ RAMÓN: Nadia and . . . If it's not too sensitive a subject: did she ever publish her novel outside of Cuba?

NADIA: No, it's a very sad story. She only brought back notes with her, just fragments of a draft . . .

ADRIANA: I read it in full, then that madwoman who was with your father stole it. She thought your mother was an upstart; there was nothing wrong with the novel at all. She wrote it for Celia, as a tribute. In the end, no one remembers her now except maybe once a year, on the anniversary of her death. Otherwise, no one even mentions her.

PAOLO B.: She was crazy too. You can mess with the monkey's chain, but don't mess with the monkey.

ALINA: But was there retaliation? Did they arrest her? It's just not clear to me what's been going on since that incident with your mother and Che at the art school.

JOSÉ RAMÓN: Whoa, stop right here. There was no incident.

ADRIANA: C'mon, let's not do this . . . Nadia, I don't know if what I'm going to tell you is fair or not. I'm two years younger than your mother, but she (*points at Mami and nudges her with her finger*) was called the First Lady because either Che was looking for her to go for a ride or Celia was on the phone for her.

MAMI: No, I was never the First Lady. If only . . .

Everyone laughs.

JOSÉ RAMÓN: That's so unfair, Adriana! Don't speak so lightly. These lies go down in history and then become myths. It wasn't like that, and I'm not going to let you tell it like that, because it's unfair. Che used to visit us all—don't speculate like that. The novel was taken away because that woman wanted something to hold over Mami . . . She tipped off the authorities, and the world came crashing down. And by the way, that woman reaped what she sowed. She's home, saying goodbye to her children as they emigrate, and making sweets to sell for dollars.

ALINA: Who was that again?

JOSÉ RAMÓN: Alondra, the journalist, whose grandfather was the minister of—

ALINA: Yes, yes, a crazy bitch. She was lovers with the entire diplomatic corps.

JOSÉ RAMÓN: The Alondra case . . . If you saw her now, you'd die. She's my neighbor. And she looks like she could be my grandmother.

ADRIANA: This woman here (*points to Mami*) could have been first in everything. She painted and wrote very well. She was a marvelous researcher . . . She was, past tense, because she's nothing now, having laid down like a carpet to be stepped on.

PAOLO B.: There are no snitches among you, are there, people who just want to fuck with you? Because I'm looking at that little friend of yours, for example, and watch out. She hasn't taken her eyes off your computer all day.

NADIA: From what I can tell, we might be a little healthier than you. For me, everyone is innocent until proven otherwise.

ALINA: Paolo, you're so bad! And as sour as ever.

ADRIANA: Look, Paolo, nobody here is going to call you in to force you to give an account of anything. So relax, sit down, and enjoy your tamale casserole.

NADIA: It seems you guys never came to any kind of agreement. I thought at this age you might have reconciled.

MAMI: There's no reconciliation on the island, just war. Lujo, our husband, did he go out? Where is he? Did he go to edit?

There is silence for a few minutes.

ADRIANA: Oh, girl, with all you've been through and you're still so stupid . . . Look at your mother: even out of her mind, she's clearer than you. Put your feet on the ground. This story has three murders to go, a bombing, and a happy ending with a hug and a smile for the camera.

ALINA: Happy ending? You really are optimistic.

PAOLO B.: I wouldn't bow my head even if I was dead. I came to see you. I want you to know that . . .

I get up from the table so as not to listen. Lujo jerks me back down. I get up again.

NADIA: I don't like soap operas. I'm going to the kitchen. I don't discuss my life at round tables.

LUJO: Nadia, c'mon, come back. Maybe he'll tell us he came to return all the paintings he stole to pay for his travels.

Collective laughter.

They talk about my mother in front of her as if she were dead. I can't stand it. I ask Dania to get off the computer so she can jot down some of what they're saying. I can't take this bunch of dilettantes anymore.

Although they're hard to follow, Dania takes notes of the fundamentals. This is nothing more than a living wake.

DANIA'S NOTES

Alina says Lujo didn't have to hand the other house over to the government, but Lujo knows you can't have two properties in Cuba. He prefers inheriting his mother's house, facing the sea, than living in an apartment full of resentments.

Adriana talks about Catullus's presence in the *Epithalamium lasciuum,* by the Dutch poet Johannes Secundus, and certain discoveries she and my mother made during those hours of sublime readings on the grass at the art school, just days before they were both expelled. All for one and one for all. They were kicked out for having an intolerable, immoral friendship. There were accusations of bisexuality. These stories all began and ended with Catullus.

Alina asks—not on her behalf, no, but on behalf of Maricela and Aleida, who write to her from Miami—if we're going to bury my mother in my father's fabulous family pantheon.

There are astonished expressions at the unexpected comment. Alina grabs her purse and goes outside to smoke. (Lujo is now American and doesn't allow smoking at home.)

Paolo B. enjoys being morbid and, all of a sudden, claims to be Nadia's father. José Ramón compares the news to the plots in nineteenth-century Cuban novels, and as if reaching a tacit agreement, they all opt for silence until some other important matter pops up. That's when Alina decides to say she's leaving for Miami, now, almost in her sixties, to start over. She doesn't want to be a radio or television presenter anymore; she says she wants to be "a person." Alina says she spends hours staring at the stove like someone detailing an abstract painting, with nothing to cook. Her life is a carbon copy of the one that ended with her mother's breakdown. She's terrified of an identical, immovable, screwed up ending. There's too much inner turmoil, yes, to be wearing darned underwear, saving detergent, walking for hours looking for transportation. So much longing without having yet turned sixty. "I'm leaving because I want to be one more person walking in the world."

"One more exile, one fewer friend," says Lujo, who's back. Everyone understands, this will now be an inner journey. Some leave; others come back.

They talk about where to buy shrimp, the official price of meat (pork), corn, Chilean wine, their fear of the coming hurricanes, and food spoiling in the refrigerator.

According to Dania's notes, my mother interjected more lucidly than the others. She said the following:

1. Common sense is the least common sense.
2. With friends like these I don't need enemies.
3. The tongue is the enemy of the body.
4. I feel guilty even when I'm not.
5. Nadia was born in 1970, and Che died in 1967.

I'd done my best. I'd dressed the round table with a linen tablecloth illustrated by Lujo more than thirty years ago. The tamale was exquisite, a dish I learned to cook by my father, who is apparently not my father anymore (but still is). Just like my house, which isn't my house, and the country that isn't my country (but still is). Or like my mother, who ran away and couldn't be my mother.

Dania and I sit at the bar that looks out a corroded window. On the high 1950s stools, we can fool ourselves into thinking we are if not bigger then at least taller than my guests. We watch them from here, like birds in flight. They look like horses at the trough, thirsty and tired from so much walking.

I'm not hungry anymore. My plate is untouched. We're no better; we no longer hope for anything. Coming in and out of the country is just a change of scenery. Cienfuegos, Paris, Havana. Not even displacement satisfies us. Traveling is another illusion.

They organized our lives and infused us with a dream of happiness. It was so real that, even though it never existed, we missed it. Were they free? Were they happy? Should they have stayed like my father? Left like my mother?

One by one, my friends leave. Paolo B. kisses me on the forehead. I feel dazed and used.

Dania and I go to bed with my mother, singing "La cleptómana." According to Lujo and my father, one of her favorite songs. While we sing, she falls asleep. We talk about recording her with us, as a trio for my show, but she couldn't follow the lyrics. We cover her and stare as she breathes, tucked between the sheets.

The Kleptomaniac

She was a kleptomaniac with beautiful baubles,
stealing for fun, for kicks, for looks.

Cute, fascinating, her misdeeds
never met a serious Court of Instruction.
I saw her one afternoon in an old shop,
stealing a whimsical little glass vial
filled with rare essences, and in her ambiguous gaze,
I got a hidden flash of the ideal.
She became my comrade for secret things,
things only women and poets know.
But her irresistible hobby reached such a point
that it wrecked my peaceful days.
She was a kleptomaniac with beautiful baubles
and she wanted to steal my heart.

"If we lived during the sixties and we were caught lying around like this, what would have happened to us?" Dania asks, yawning.

"I wouldn't have been able to take all that. My mother's a martyr."

"You love her?"

"We're just getting to know each other."

Dania falls asleep. I look at the notes she wrote on a piece of a grocery bag. Paolo B. was right: my friend was trained to take notes in shorthand. She's quick, sagacious, and a snitch.

I can't sleep. The phone rings; a phone ringing at dawn, the worst noise in the world. It's José Ramón, who can't sleep either. I invite him to breakfast tomorrow. He wants to tell me about my mother's book. He's the one who can help me, he says. What an unusual inheritance of friends she's left me! In each of them I discover what I've lost.

BREAKFAST, THE FISHBOWL, AND MY MOTHER'S DEATH

The sea looked like a steaming bowl of soup.

That morning I set the table on the terrace that faces the Malecón; the white linen tablecloth flutters beautifully along the blue shoreline. People always pass by and look, which is why I don't usually like to eat here, because of the looks. But in a struggle between the sea and these witnesses, the sea always wins. I don't want to deprive us of breakfast in the open air.

Café con leche and bread with butter. Guava jam and mango juice. José Ramón arrives while I am settling Mami.

In fifteen minutes we are having breakfast. Mami stays in bed, as usual, after her morning bath.

NOTES FROM MY DIALOGUE WITH JOSÉ RAMÓN

"I ASKED about your mother's book because I've always felt guilty about what happened to her. Of all of us, the only one who could have done something was me. I was, let's say, the most reliable. If I'd kept the original, like she asked me, it'd be a published book. Things have changed a lot; the pyramid has been inverted. My two sons are in Spain and now I find myself offering them explanations, arguments, about why I continue to be a member of the Party. Can you imagine the madness of it all? My children don't understand my position. But that's how I'm going to die, Nadia.

"Lujo told me you plan to rewrite the book. I want to help you. You led a different life. We neither attacked the Moncada nor enjoyed a brief breath of freedom. Our fate has been to be stuck between two streams. But if I can help, let me know.

"Do you remember Pucha? That is, Ana Irma. (Your mother gave everybody nicknames.) We're neighbors; we do the nightly watch together on our block. We've been friends for more than twenty years. I'll bring you the interview I did a few months ago, when I found out from Lujo that your mother was coming back. I asked if she'd finally published the novel about Celia, although I was referring to a different version, because the original never left Cuba. Here are my notes on the conversation with the person who was closest to Celia in her last years. Use it for that book—that's why I'm giving these to you. Rewrite it from your perspective. Don't let this get lost. Investigate."

"What my mother brought with her are pieces, delusions, fragments of what could have been and isn't," I tell him. "I'd have to do so much research. I don't know if they'd let me publish that here; they might ask me why I'm interviewing people, and then history would repeat itself."

"It's not the same as before, Nadia. Everything's changing. It's why I believe in this country. You think that if something could happen to you I'd push you to write about Celia?"

"I'm grateful to you, José Ramón, but right now all my mother's fears have spilled into me."

"Well, no, that's the one thing about her you have to discard. I'm asking you as if you were my daughter."

"Why did you guys show up so late?"

"Some because of fear and others because of your father, who terrorized anyone who brought up your mother's name. I listened to your programs, I followed you every night on the radio and warned you about the crazy things you were doing; I was the listener who sent you letters: Eduardo and family, remember . . . ?"

At the Malecón a group of people are shouting. We try to continue our conversation, but suddenly a fire truck pulls up. Lujo sits down to have breakfast with us. The tumult is strange. We try to talk about the interview with Pucha, but each time the screams get louder.

Lujo says my mother wanted to name me Celia but that it didn't go well with my father's battle cry of a surname (Guerra means war). I'm surprised. We try to ignore the rabble so as not to get involved in what's happening across the street. We have no questions and are just trying to go on . . . but it's too much. I get up and go to the gate. I lean over to watch although there's nothing in particular to see, only that the crowd's growing larger. We don't want to cross the street; everything suggests a tragedy. We stay quiet, watching the spectacle from our balcony. The drama intensifies as more on-lookers gather. Apparently the firefighters can't do anything. We only hear: "Someone's drowned," "Someone's drowned." Someone's always drowning on the Malecón. Lujo wants to cross the street, but we tell him to have his breakfast in peace.

Suddenly a neighbor comes running, yanks open the gate, and screams: "It's her, Lujo, run."

I knew it. I knew it. It is my mother. She launched herself into the sea. Like a fish stuck between rocks, like a rafter who's surrendered, like one of many suicidal poets, guided by the broken compass of her madness. All this tumult is for my mother. Lujo screams like a woman in the delivery room; José Ramón leaps to the opposite side of the sidewalk and runs away without a glance back. I reach out to touch her.

She threw herself into the water because the sea is a steaming bowl of soup, just as I noticed before breakfast. Or she came to die and, in a moment of lucidity, regained her self-confidence and decided to end her tragedy in a big way. She died like an old Eskimo woman, preferring not to walk back and have to step on the waters; she never looked back.

I recognize her beautiful body, drowned, wasted, but hers. There is no doubt. This is my mother.

Everything happened while we had breakfast. While life went on, quietly. This is the fishbowl of death, and I'm constantly in this fishbowl. I could have kept this from happening, and yet I considered it, at first, just a spectacle intruding on my life. This time it was someone of mine who drowned; I should have been paying attention.

How the simplest things happen in this world. That's how alien life was with my mother, always through third parties, even her death. Why should I have expected any other ending? It was like a film being shown to me—and that involves me—but without my having the right to challenge the narrative. My God, if you can, give me a better role in this plot; let me decide something, however minimal. I just want to act for myself sometime.

FAREWELL AND MOURNING, FOR MY MOTHER

My mother's friends gather in Lenin Park. This park was one of Celia's projects. My mother brought me here several times while it was being built. She would lie on the grass and smoke for hours. I'd run around and hide in the trees. This is where I decided to spread her ashes, on the grass.

Where were we when she forgot the first word? And is there anyone who can give me any information about her? Who said running away would dispel her fears? Who were the accessories to that fear? When did she first fail to recognize me?

Even here, Cuba continues to be a lost shore, unreachable.

She was a Protestant and a Marxist, a Cuban and an American, a literacy teacher and a painter, addicted to Led Zeppelin and Los Compadres. She was the muse for certain songs from the '70s. She's portrayed in paintings and photos that immortalize her.

Her poems, letters, and notes speak of a talent dispersed in anonymity.

Who can say an official farewell to a hippie like her, a

stranger to me, an old friend to so many of you? I didn't have time to get to know her as I would have liked.

We aren't able to thank her or apologize to her. Let's quote a friend: "Silence, a bird has died."

I'm going to read this poem by my mother, the one that's most her. This is how I want to remember her.

Science Fiction

And if a green man came
and if a green or blue man came
in a spaceship.
And if he came.
What would he say about me, so disheveled,
without frills or grace.
What would he say about everyone because of me.

WE'VE GROWN

Diego's letter in my red diary.

Nadia:
Your letter has left me speechless. Nothing I could
write will bring you comfort. I don't want to mourn
her death; crying would drain me of the strength to
get to you. I'm farther away than I'd like, but I'm going
to stop everything to be with you. You can't continue
locked up like your mother or you'll end up going
crazy. C'mon, get out, walk to the beach. Get some sun
and rest that salty body until I can get there and love
you a little.

I want to call you, but I know you don't like hearing
me from far away. It's very early; I'm sure you're asleep.
I'm wandering around Europe; I've been working
and trying to get ahead. I want to be there. To stop
everything and take you away.

For the moment: I'll bring you mint tea with orange
blossom in bed, caress your bare feet. There's fresh bread.
You can sit up a little, let your neck show. Butter,
blackberry jam, a kiss on your navel to start the day.

You wake up, the light is on . . . Go to the sea and wait for me there.

Your Diego

Dear Diego:
I only turn on the computer to write to you. The only thing left for me is to talk to you. I don't know if I can still float. It's dangerous for me to get close to the water. Sometimes I want to sink; I weigh too much to stay on the surface. I want to be anchored. I can't take it anymore. So many deaths make me weak.

I'm not a fictional character.

I need you. Come.

Nadia

P.S. I'm listening to your advice. Starting tomorrow, I'll go to the beach near here, because I'm waiting for you.

Nadia:
Yesterday I called your house and Lujo told me you don't want to eat. I'm already in Mexico; when you least expect it, I'll be in Havana. I don't want a woman torn apart by tears; when I get there, I want to love you in all your beauty.

I beg you to listen to me. Take a deep breath, chew, swallow, sleep, swim, live. I'd do anything to get you to eat dinner, at least tonight.

For starters, I'd serve you tortilla soup with avocado, pasilla chili, pork rinds, cream, and fresh cheese, then mole (it can be the traditional poblano mole or a very good melon one), and we can conclude with chongos zamoranos while we toast with an excellent Mexican stone wine. I'll bite your bare shoulder (because you have to be bare shouldered).

Although, on second thought, I want to taste all your spices. Lujo tells me you're a very good cook. I'll rid myself of everything and go find you in Cuba, you, only you, only for you . . .

Yours,
Diego

JULY 28

I'm going to La Concha, a completely run-down club on the coast, an empty shell of what it was once: our happiness ten summers ago.

Still standing is the old diving board the lifeguards used to paint aqua blue. There's the old chaise, sitting in the sun, where I used to surrender to teenage boys swollen with desire. My body opened the dam to let their hot sperm pass, the colossal fighters: "the golden masks . . ."

None of that survives. I don't know where those extras from my '90s movie have gone. Everybody who laughed when they watched me compete, small and frail, against the handsome lifeguard doing triple somersaults until I felt faint, brushing against the breakwaters, victorious or defeated in that delirium that comes from trying to beat the biggest barbarian.

This is all history, Nadia. Now we're going to clear our minds and feel the currents between our legs. Cold currents, icy currents, warm currents, hot currents—the past never travels in these channels that sweep us along.

Stop, Nadia. Stop, please, you tell yourself. Stop or you'll die. You knowme-Iknowmyself-youknowyourself I'm an idea machine, me, myself, Nadia. This is how I'm (we're) killing me.

My right foot pushes to ease the tension on the board.

My head imagines a ship labeled *Mediterranean*. I raise my chin until I can't read anything. Standing straight, I hear the creaking of the rusty spring. I'm in the air, hovering over a mirror of salt. I measure the slimy algae at the bottom and breathe in, calculating the distance to a few yellow fish, and in a rush of clarity, I inhale the air I'll need, sigh and rise as only my mother's mad spirit could rise . . .

I smile as I try to make a perfect arrow out of my spine. I can't stop thinking, I'm always scheming, but when I'm already arched and up high, very high, tucking my knees, vaulting into the sky, I see Diego in a suit and tie standing in front of me. I fall into the water knowing that was no vision. Triple reverse somersault and Diego under the sea. Diego among urchins and rust. Diego saves me from being anchored. Diego has jumped into the water to rescue me.

Women who live on islands always need a savior, thus so many great historical confusions. Choosing the right savior to free ourselves takes years; sometimes it's best not to be rescued.

I want to live here with him, under the sea. It's unusual for a Cuban woman to really want a foreign body so much, but Diego has already lost his nationality; his body tastes like Cuba and his voice houses all accents.

The best part of summer is feeling this man dressed and wet in my arms. Crazed, his neck hot, his tie floating alongside us, we rescue ourselves, together.

He strips me of my fear of life, his gestures sanctify me, his sensuality makes death go away, and then a potent Diego enters me. In the water, we're all the same, simple animals dripping with desire. We are my hips and his thighs, my neck and his bite. The hook of his erect sex is my bait. I bite and swallow its bittersweet milk along with the salt of this deranged Caribbean.

Diego throws me up against the seawall, so only his strong knees support me in front of the diving board, now split apart. He penetrates me in a series of contractions of water and light. I only suffer and suffer until I laugh; he pushes the pain out of me. The surface doesn't exist, only his sex and mine sending bubbles between the depths and the light, between the white end and the mighty turquoise. Mollusks, fish, creatures come as Diego arranges them on this slippery body tied to him by pain and lust.

Diego cries as he comes, furiously, and we wave goodbye to our childhood. Diego takes me under as I finish my leap from the diving board to ecstasy. I jab and stretch, slip through the waters as if I could fill the sea with my fluids. The summer of my life is under the sea.

Diego is here! Let the ships decapitate the waves. The only desire that satisfies me is here.

His tears sparkle in the sun. My back bleeds, but for the first time, not a single red drop leaves my sex.

The best thing about the tropics is feeling the ships passing over our heads while we anchor just off Cuba's territorial waters, not seen or suspected, secret and silent like the Russian submarines slithering under the skirt of the socialist Caribbean. Diego is finally here, and his revolution in my body is the only thing that really matters.

HOW WE GOT THE NEWS (II)

JULY 31

Everything was already dead.

I didn't want to save anything for the future; I was on edge. I was still afflicted with the Scarlett O'Hara syndrome, but my fear of poverty had managed to appease it with so many deaths. The dark under my eyes looked like a cursed black butterfly. I was also a little dead.

The death foretold of someone close alienates you from ambition, from selfishness, even from the anxiety over what's going to happen tomorrow. You live for now, today; you stay still, like someone waiting to hear the hunter fire his shot just before the hare bolts.

Coming home from the beach that day, Diego told me the people who greeted him on the streets of Havana seemed like ghosts from the past. That every trip to Cuba was like being in a black-and-white movie. I want to live with Diego, but on that Cuba–Mexico route, could we keep our desire alive? Has anyone lived these last fifty years between countries without losing the thread of passion? I don't know if it's possible. Many families get lost trying. I can't abandon Diego. And I don't know how to live without Cuba.

Everything was already dead for me, and that morning, while Lujo continued to inventory paintings and valuables I should keep for the future, I felt alien and disturbed. It's just that none of these things belonged to me. They weren't part of my childhood, or part of my family. I was listless, blank. My body and soul marched independent of each other. These deaths were also killing Diego. He told me so as he was leaving. Now it was just the two of us, Lujo and me, the house and the phone.

My friend Fabián called, one of my former classmates waiting for his visa for the Guggenheim grant.

"The good news is we got multiple entry visas, and we can go to the United States any time we want."

I wasn't happy, nor was it clear to me that I wanted to go on with the project I'd prepared for the grant. I told Lujo.

For him, it was sad news; so many months without me would be a nightmare. We were alone, and this time it was a deep loneliness, because we didn't have expectations anymore about being saved from our isolation. Those who should still be with us had left us too soon.

"Why aren't we happy? Any Cuban would jump with joy and toast that news. I don't really feel anything. Not happiness, not sadness," I said.

Lujo was taking notes. He put the pencil over his ear and looked at me over his glasses.

"I'll tell you, as your mother would say, quoting Darío, the fatalist: 'Blessed is the tree that's barely sensitive / and even more blessed the hard stone because it no longer feels'."

At around five in the afternoon, while I was watering my plants and thinking of cooking something light, three vintage American cars drove up to the house. The passengers were former classmates. They asked me to go with them to Cojímar. They were celebrating our trip to New York. Lujo encouraged me to get out of the house. It was us, again: time had dispersed us after we left school, but now it'd brought us together after my mother's death.

I'm going with Fabián in a '57 Chevrolet restored by his grandfather; Ana and Alejandro are in another car, a flamingo-pink color. The caboose is Julio, with his headphones on, at the wheel of a '58 Buick.

Every time I see Julio I get butterflies in my stomach. He's the most sensual and troubled guy I've ever met, but I tell myself: "Don't go back to the places where you were once happy." We had an affair at school, something he doesn't seem to remember, something I can't forget but masterfully conceal. I smother the butterflies in my stomach; I kill them so I can be a woman of the world, who ignores everything other than listening to music, driving, and doing her work.

We go through La Bahía Tunnel, which boasts origins in the '50s—aqua-green tiles, the smells of shellfish and fermentation. We finally reach the terrace in Cojímar, where Hemingway always ended up drinking with the local fishermen after hunting their sea beasts. I said it felt like a trip to the past. I made them look at my skirt, and at Fabian's shoes, as retro as his recycled car.

They ignored me, argued about cocktails, name dropped New York restaurants, passed gallery phone numbers among themselves, and ordered exotic drinks. They ceased being present; they'd left. I was still anchored to the ground. I spent the afternoon holding the same glass of red wine.

I went out to the terrace, went down the steps to look at

the coast, the rust-covered bottom at my feet. I can't live without these places. All this is me; it contains me. What can I say to Diego? I don't want to leave forever. None of my classmates tried to cheer me up; they were busy being happy. I wanted to continue my goodbyes, to continue mourning until I was drained.

As evening fell, schools of sardines drew silver circles in the sea. A humid air was blowing, overwhelming me. I went up to the restaurant again. My friends were laughing and sketching out installation projects on their napkins. Fishermen and simple people passed by and peeked in on us in our delirium. I felt guilty. I'm very fragile.

Something is changing, I thought. What am I doing here?

In the evening, we ordered soup and rice with seafood. Julio hugged me tightly, led me to the terrace, our bodies dangling dangerously over the cliff, the sea below us. Almost in the water, held back only by the window's glass.

"I've never forgotten you, you know," he whispered. "I don't know why I haven't tried to see you, but I feel like if I do, I'll go to ruin. How about you?"

"I try, but you can't live on past passions."

We both laughed, hugging each other. We kissed, a tender and inoffensive kiss.

We went back to our table. Almost everyone was drunk, though I hadn't tasted anything other than that first glass of wine. I'd just squeezed the lemon into my soup when our waiter came and asked us kindly to leave, right now, that we didn't have to pay for the food, just the drinks. We were stunned.

"What happened? What did we do?"

We thought it was a game.

"I can't explain it. Go to the bar and look at the TV," the waiter said, picking up the bowls of soup.

The line to get in the bar was eternal.

"Watch the next newscast," the waiter advised. "Fidel has resigned."

He'd been sick.

I saw people with watery eyes, wry smiles, fear, strangeness, shock. I couldn't see myself in the confusion. We paid our bill in silence. Nobody dared say a word. We were a group of young people born and raised listening to the same president's speeches all our lives. Ever since we could remember, we hadn't experienced anyone else in charge of the country. We thought that would never come. We kissed and said goodbye without questions. As we left, the restaurant was closing, the back doors and windows already locked.

We went in a caravan of silence back along the same 1950s road, but in reverse. We skirted the cold, dark coastline. On the Malecón, people weren't staring at the water but at the empty city.

Once we got to my house, Fabián took my hand.

"What's going to happen?"

"For the moment, nothing. Take care," I said fondly, and we hugged. "I don't know when we'll see each other again."

In the house, Lujo was pure nerves. He asked the same question, and as if an oracle were speaking. Again I said: "Nothing's going to happen for now, so you can start by calming yourself down. Do you want a café con leche? I haven't eaten anything."

We drank our café con leches in silence. In front of the

house, the same sea. People quietly returned to their homes, and that night Nadia, in her role as oracle, could not sleep a wink. The phone wouldn't stop ringing: Diego, friends of Lujo and my father—they wanted to know if we were still alive.

I woke up several times, and at dawn I finally gave up. I decided to jot down some notes in my notebook. While day broke, I wrote: "In my country all roads lead to Fidel: what you eat, what you wear, the blackouts, your rent, schools, trips, promotions, demotions, cyclones, epidemics, carnivals, congresses, roads. Very few important things have happened without him. Today, sitting in front of the TV, I said to myself (with a little more clarity than Lujo): 'Nothing is going on here but life itself.' The streets are quiet, the people sitting on the Malecón stare at the city where nothing seems to have changed. Something is ending, but I can't figure out what."

My friends would be flying to New York very soon. My head flew in another direction. I had another pending matter. There was no time to lose. Death traveled alongside me.

NOTE

Lujo puts me in touch with Lourdes Argibay, Celia's niece and friend for many years. She agrees to give us her testimony. The talk is emotional but calm. According to Lujo, Lourdes is who most reminds him of Celia physically. Writing a book is a serious endeavor, but finding the real Celia is complicated. She didn't want to leave a trace, she's been erased, and we vanish as soon as we look for her.

LETTERS, LETTERS, LETTERS

My dear Diego:
I recently read a transcript of the postcard Che sent to
his wife Aleida March while at the Louvre Museum. I
thought about sending you my notes after reading it. I
think about the distant and cold hero, not the husband
of that woman who waits and waits and waits forever, I
think even still. I don't know if that can ever be outdone.
Now everything seems simpler: he's just a man buying
a postcard for his wife, writing, filling in the card in
a corner under a yellow light at the museum, writing
certain words that say I love you without saying it.
He's not someone I understand. I've been tortured by
a misunderstanding of the hero figure since childhood.
Every morning I swore (we swore) to be like him, and
now I read this distant or endearing postcard from the
human being, the lover, and I don't know, I can't know
who he really was beyond his marble statue. It's the first
time I've had a document in my hand that makes me
question the lives of these immovable beings from our
childhood. My love, read carefully. It's written on the
back of a reproduction of a portrait of Lucrezia Crivelli,
painted by Leonardo da Vinci.

My dear:
Dreaming of holding hands with you in the Louvre, I saw you represented there, curvy, serious, with a slightly sad smile (perhaps because nobody loves you), waiting for the distant beloved (is it who I think or someone else?).

I let go of your hand to see you better and guess what you've hidden in your prodigal bosom. Male, right? A kiss and a big hug for everyone and especially for you.

from
Mariscal Thu Che

Aleida and Ernesto's third daughter was named Celia. My mother thought of naming me Celia too, but my surname didn't match the ideals the name inspired in her. My concern for her, for the stolen novel, and all those other things haunt me, reinforcing an idea: I have to go to Miami with the visa and my grant money. I'll spend a weekend with Celia's relatives. I'd like to finish my mother's book. I don't want to just sit here; the journey's already begun. It's better this way. Lujo will call you and let you know when I've landed, when they've come to get me; these are people who've helped us a lot. Tell me when you can come so we can schedule our times and decide what to do with our lives. I adore you. You've given me so much strength.

Your Nadia Guerra

Nadia:

I'm calling you this afternoon so we can decide on the dates. I can't go to Miami with you for the usual reasons, work. When you fly back to Cuba, I want to be waiting for you at the airport. Let's talk calmly, and I'll take you with me to write "your mother's book" in peace. Don't leave the phone off the hook. I'll call you late, very late, at the end of my show. Kisses everywhere.

Diego

WHAT IS A CUBAN WOMAN?

As I prepare to pack my suitcase—it's only for a few days—I notice the clothes my mother had been wearing. I wonder what we're made of, what feelings I have about being who I am, about who we are at the end of everything. I open the suitcase and pray.

Swimsuits drying out in the sun, black tears, reverb, dancing a sad conga in flip-flops, rouge, methylene blue, house robes, fried eggs, pain and forgiveness, a friend's clothes, eyes made up in haste, clothes on a Caribbean body, lost letters, long hair in rollers, violet water, violet skin exposed to the sun, butter suntan lotion, carmine in the mirrors, sandals full of sand, a little mug in the bathroom for washing, suspicion, machismo Leninism, crying after an orgasm, tickling from sex, "Babe, do you love me?" Silent intelligence; cooking while barefoot between blackouts; legs extended on the floor after cleaning, mobilized, summoned; head wrapped in a kerchief; the battalion marching and almost dancing; a woman working with her daughter playing next to her. Listening to Radio Reloj reports while putting on makeup, laughing sadly, café con leche and bread and butter, a bath with white flowers and husks, eucalyptus breaths, rice and beans in the pressure cooker, to feel, to speak, to explode, a collective birth, sex on bunk beds, homemade sanitary pads, crazy academics dancing, housewife philosophers, Los Van Van, goodbye and rice, Caribbean-born Penelopes, a relaxed depth, fried ripe plantains, nudist camping, the black-and-white portrait from a *quinces* party, getting married in three days, divorce Cuban-style, happy tears, flowers for Ochún, desire, desire, wishes to be fulfilled, Russian boots, guerrilla miniskirts, ardor and salt, simple prayers under a cloud of speeches.

In the crowd we're unique, first ladies lost in the rabble.

JOURNEY TO MIAMI

I was four hours early to the airport. I'd been warned the process would be long.

The bureaucracy was more complicated than the flight. So close yet so far. There's barely any time between takeoff and landing; forty minutes in the air and we're on the other side.

People travel in silence to meet their past or their future. Tense, thoughtful, red-eyed, and furrow-browed. Do they always leave someone or something behind? A child is crying. On landing, people crowd the windows to look out at a sea of fireflies. "The light, brother, the light."

The sightseers disembark first. Political prisoners and immigrants wait for officials while still on the plane. It seems incredible that the paperwork takes so much longer than the flight itself.

No one was waiting for me. I knew this would be the case, but seeing so many people hugging excitedly made me feel a little jealous, a little empty and scared about what to expect.

I'm only here for four short days, I thought, four days under the gun. If I start calling people, I'll unleash the past, so I'd rather just interview Celia's sister, see the few people Lujo found for me, and leave.

My friend Raffaello Fornés, who already knew I was coming, was waiting for me at my sweet little hotel on the beach.

He's very discreet and only talks about architecture and yoga; he doesn't care much for politics or where you decide to live. We had dinner together and he told me about Havana and Miami; he wanted to give me his perspective on both cities. We went for a walk in Miami Beach. The night was cool and Fornés was trying to evoke a bridge between the two shores.

"Miami's not a city: it's a region. It's the second Cuban settlement, after Havana. And only forty-five minutes by plane from the most Fidelist island of Cuba. Let's compare Miami to dense, run-down Havana. Miami's the only city in the hemisphere where an unprecedented urban phenomenon is happening: it's growing inward. In the meantime, urban expansion, like in North America, has invaded Europe and the rest of the world. Miami also has a great technological infrastructure."

I listened attentively to his long theories about Miami and Havana: the yin and yang of cities. The Cuban part of Miami is a reflection of Havana, with the same names for restaurants, the flavors, the smells, people staring at your shoes, just like in El Vedado. We've built ourselves a small ghetto reflection, the city and its mirror, the expansion of another city ninety miles beyond the island itself, with thousands of replicants driving along the roads at the edge of the sea, perhaps with the strange illusion that these might end at the Malecón in Havana. If you squint your eyes and take a breath, if you listen to the voices and close your eyes a little, just a little, it can seem like you're still in Cuba.

Walking Miami's streets with Raffaello, I feel safe. In the days that follow, we walk to many places. We went to his house on the beach, which is very Zen, spacious, sunny, and essential in its decoration. Then we walked around several places I don't want to forget: Lincoln Road Mall and the South Beach art deco district, Vizcaya Museum and Gardens, the Biltmore Hotel in Coral Gables. I had to deliberately keep my mind open for everything to register.

Raffaello had a single topic of conversation: Havana and Miami, two points that seem so far apart but might be the same place.

CAFÉ NOSTALGIA

TONIGHT I went out with Pepe Horta, whom I already knew through my father from when he did an exquisite annual program and threw lovely parties at the New Latin American Film Festival in Havana. How could I forget his black eyes and his exuberant laugh, his excellent French and his pointed opinions on everything in the world?

As I was crossing the street to the beach, right there in the middle of traffic, his funny jeep rescued me from the lights and merriment of night in Miami Beach. Pepe is a friend of Lujo's, and he met my mother during the hard years. Because she was younger than all of them, he remembers very little about her; she, my mother, is like a shadow in his memory.

Pepe's the only person who's done something really useful with nostalgia: created a place to sing it, dance it, party with it, and enjoy it. Café Nostalgia to feel, Café Nostalgia to relive—with joy—the past composed of each and every one of us.

When we arrived, the place was still empty, and everything smelled and tasted of Havana. It's a casual, easy place that promises the best is yet to come . . .

The waiters are like a big family. The dancers, ghosts from the past, come in one by one. I know some of them by reference; others worked as actors in my father's films. I also run into many of my friends; it's Pepe who's engineered all this, because nostalgia, when it's good, doesn't kill but sustains and saves us.

I danced with so many different parts of my culture: a little Afro-Cuba, a pinch of La Lupe, some arpeggios from Lecuona, the best of Los Van Van, Irakere, Elena Burke, all of it played live courtesy of the Café Nostalgia orchestra.

At dawn Pepe took me to his house, not to show me photos of my father in Paris, or to tell me sad stories about what he left in Havana, no. Pepe just wanted to offer me a Cuban café con leche with a pinch of salt before sunrise . . . When we woke up, we had breakfast together. His art collection is a real throwback to my parents' time, to the Cuba I'd like to save from disaster.

Pepe has a very special project; he wants to sell everything, including his club. He wants to go live in his house in El Vedado with his mother and perhaps create a spiritual retreat in Viñales.

The previous night Pepe gave me a gift: he revealed the difference between nostalgia and melancholia. One is played with a violin, the other with a guitar. Melancholia pulls us to the bottom, but nostalgia is a stepping stone to the next stage in our lives.

This place could be that too, depending on the protagonist and her style when playing the piano keys of life.

It's funny. Pepe is one of the few people in Miami who's not afflicted with Miami's most common disease: nostalgia.

At daybreak, Pepe drops me off at my little hotel on the

beach, I go up the stairs, look at the sea, and close the curtains so I can sleep . . .

It smells of dry docks here, of shellfish on the coast of Miramar, of burnt butter at the *playita* on Sixteenth Street, of my house the last time Lujo brewed coffee. Nostalgia is an endemic disease from which I don't want to save myself.

CHELA'S HOUSE

CELIA'S ONLY living sister, Chela, left Cuba at the beginning of the Revolution. Today she is turning ninety years old. Memories mingle in her head. She's sweet, elegant, and delicate. Celia looked a lot like her sisters, so I imagine this is how Celia would have aged.

It was a coincidence that my trip fell on her birthday. Lujo managed to get me invited to her birthday party, and here I was. Cuba was very far away at this gathering, and yet it was the pretext for everything. In her short and scattered speech, Chela talked about her sisters; Celia and Acacia Norma, Aca's mother, were special to her, and she spoke in present and past tense about them. There were many gaps, and little by little her memory failed. People clapped excitedly, celebrated, danced to Cuban music made in Miami and also to Cuban music made in Cuba, as if there was nothing unusual here. No blockade, no political discussions. It was a Cuban party in Kendall.

We danced until very late. We shared anecdotes, connected names, common places in Havana from before and now, my father's films, art galleries, and well-known exhibitions. They made a warm place for me, where I seemed to have lived even while living across the waters. That night I was able to break the horizon's line, where so many rafters, martyrs, heroes, separations, landslides, seemed to blur by the second, but then reappear when I remembered I was there on loan. Was I a spy? Was I just curious? Who had brought me here? What was I doing here?

Just evoking Lujo Rojas's name helped everything fall into place, so the important thing was to keep on going, drawing undue attention to the crossfire between the island and Miami. This was the best thing I learned on this trip, to tiptoe, to try to be quiet and listen. Our emotions always go to where we're most spiritually comfortable. Wherever they land, that's where we go. Beyond politics or geography.

When dinner was served, a very elegant man came over to tell us about the black beans, and thinking I was born outside of Cuba, he began to offer details about the original flavors of the dishes, mentioning things I'd never even tried in Cuba. What dishes and what island was he talking about? What he was narrating didn't exist. It was obvious he never realized I was a Cuban who lived in Cuba. That's always a good question: What's a Cuban from Cuba like? What are the differences between inxile and exile?

At the party I took notes on my conversations with the rest of the family. I was able to meet Acacia (Aca) Gloria Gómez Sánchez, "La Pompa," Marcos Gómez Sánchez, "Chongolo," the children of Acacia Norma Sánchez Manduley and Delio Gómez Ochoa (commander of the Sierra Maestra). I want my mother's book to have all of its protagonists' contradictions; I don't want a predictable book. I want to expose our internal struggles, our pain, and our proximity to Cuba's saga. I intend to write it in the next few months, with as many dimensions as the subject of Cuba allows.

FIDEL'S LITTLE GIRL

LUJO IS also friends with Alina Fernández, Fidel's first and only daughter.

There are many stories about her. It's said she escaped from Cuba disguised in a blond wig, that Fidel never took care of her, that her mother, Natalia F. Revueltas, was never the First Lady either.

Why did she never use the Castro surname? What are Fidel's intimate relationships with women like? How was his relationship with his only daughter, now a mature woman?

All the answers are there, on the map of her childhood, which took place during the first stage of the Revolution, when Fidel made his home at Celia Sánchez's house.

Alina welcomed me politely and with kindness to her lovely home in Miami. She's an intelligent and beautiful woman. Talking with her was a real journey to the center of the problem: Fidel and his relationships with women.

ALINA: When I was born, the Revolution hadn't triumphed yet. I'm making a confession about an unforgivable age. We had a very stable family life. I ate sitting in a high chair. I remember one day I choked on orange juice. I remember the trips to the park. It was a totally different time. We lived at Fifteenth and Fourth in El Vedado. It was a big house, with seven bedrooms, a house belonging to upper-middle-class professionals. My mother was married to Dr. Orlando Fernández Ferrer, who was a cardiologist. My mother worked at Esso as chief of staff. I'm trying to explain that we were working people. In Cuba, our serenity was disturbed by Batista's coup, which was opposed by a good part of Cuban society. People were against it because we were a republic that was just beginning to deal with its flaws.

NADIA: How did it affect you as a child? We're talking about the first few years of your life.

ALINA: What children feel are the atmospherics, the moods, the emotions of those around them. And that was very evident to me, since I was a child. There was indifference, worry, happiness . . . so many emotions in our home because, in addition to the family, there were people who worked at our house, and, well, all that changed one fine day with the triumph of the Revolution.

NADIA: Did you feel that this doctor, Orlando Fernández, was your father?

ALINA: We had this tradition. I remember our front door was frosted, double glass, and he would open it—I'd be waiting for him and would run into his arms. I remember running while still in diapers, running, running, running.

NADIA: How old were you?

ALINA: A year. But I have memories from the cradle. He had a clinic at the house. There was a fluorescent lamp, and he'd sit his patients in front of it, and you could see their heart beat. It was like discovering a different world. I loved being there, in his office. I believe that's why I fell in love with medicine and why it's what I studied. All that changed (my memory is totally visual) when, instead of Donald Duck and Mickey Mouse cartoons, TV began to show advancing— that's what they were doing—bearded men hanging off Sherman tanks, with their guns and necklaces and all that. I think they were driving toward Havana for, like, eight days, and then one night the main bearded guy showed up in our living room. From then on, everything fell apart. My life changed like the life of the country, very abruptly.

NADIA: Did the doctor know you weren't his daughter?

ALINA: Yes, he knew.

NADIA: Did you call him "Dad"?

ALINA: You know, I don't really remember, but I'm sure I did. I was telling you my parents met in the context of conspiracy and opposition to Batista. My mother had given keys to the house to the three main emerging leaders of the rebel forces.

NADIA: So he used that key to come into the house?

ALINA: Yes, but look . . . Fidel entered Havana on January 8th, but as far as I was concerned, he leapt from the TV screen into our living room.

NADIA: Was that the first time you met? What do you remember about this moment?

ALINA: I remember cigar smoke. I remember a very big person. I remember a gift he brought me: a baby doll like those we'd had before, but this one was dressed like him, like Fidel, with hair stuck on his face, a beard . . . That toy was his alter ego.

NADIA: When you saw him for the first time, were you impressed by the uniform? Were you impressed by his height?

ALINA: No, I don't remember being impressed at all. I believe what children want is to be held; anything can make them happy. I remember I peeled the hair off the doll's face.

NADIA: He'd gone to see your mother and the doctor, to talk to them?

ALINA: I imagine he was there to talk to them.

NADIA: And the doctor? Your sister? What happened to them?

ALINA: We moved out of the house, and my father and my sister began to fade a bit.

NADIA: Were there plans for you to move in with Fidel?

ALINA: Well, I didn't have any plans. That was a question for the adults—I was just a girl.

NADIA: Wasn't it traumatic to move with your mother and leave the doctor, whom you saw as your father? You talk about this very casually.

ALINA: No, because we moved to a fabulous place in front of the *playita* at Sixteenth Street, a lovely place for children, because when you went down the stairs, there was a natural pool off the rocks. Next door, the neighbors had a lion and a monkey as pets. They belonged to the owner of the Sierra Maestra building (the former Rosita de Hornedo hotel), and he was always very generous with children.

NADIA: Didn't you miss your sister and the man you'd known as your father?

ALINA: Children adapt very easily. I don't remember missing him. And everything was so traumatic anyway. Also, right about then they'd enrolled me in a school I hated with all my heart. Pediatricians always say that if you're going to make a change, like changing a kid's pacifier, for example, just do it.

NADIA: So that was your exile to the beach, without your first father and sister?

ALINA: Yes, it was very abrupt. Perhaps if we'd stayed in the other house the absence would have been more noticeable.

NADIA: So at the time, it was just your Tata, your mother, and the sea?

ALINA: Well, Fidel visited late at night, always very late, but that ended at a certain point.

NADIA: When did you become aware of your family again?

ALINA: The truth is I had a family for a very short time. At that time in Cuba, if you had a relative or someone very close who'd left Cuba, it was highly stigmatized, and you had to report it.

NADIA: When you started at this school, did your classmates know who your parents were?

ALINA: After three days or a week everyone knew . . .

NADIA: Everyone except you.

ALINA: Except me. Just an innocent walking through life. But yes, little by little I realized what was happening because it was very obvious. Children tell everything. Children repeat everything they hear at home.

NADIA: With all the political fervor of the Revolution in education and the centrality of Fidel in the schools—the Pioneers wrote compositions and odes to Fidel; the murals featured him; he was in the morning papers, in political songs, everywhere. When that happened, didn't it occur to you to tell your friends Fidel was visiting your mother?

ALINA: Well, people knew. Slowly I began to understand, but very slowly.

NADIA: Did you ever wonder why Fidel came to visit?

ALINA: No. The truth is, his visits were very pleasant. He was great at playing children's games, especially games that involved his hands. And it was so late. He'd come at the small hours of the morning. I loved it.

NADIA: What did you play with him?

ALINA: Jacks and pick-up-sticks.

NADIA: At what point did you find out he was your father? Did you hear it from the doctor?

ALINA: No, no, he wouldn't have had a chance to tell me—remember, back then, everyone who left was a traitor. I never heard from him again. Remember that we lived obsessed with everything the "neighbor across the street" was doing; there was no communication. Everyone was leaving. There was always a reason to leave, to not be there.

NADIA: So you were ten when your mother decided to talk to you about this. Do you remember how the conversation went with your mother about your true parent?

ALINA: I don't remember it very well, but she had a very interesting room—a room like a suite. Before you were actually in the house proper there was, like, a living room. It had a small sofa, a recliner, a record player. It was very nice, and you could talk there. It must have been like that. But it didn't surprise me at all.

NADIA: Why not?

ALINA: It didn't surprise me because you feel things or know them already. I believe children have an overdeveloped instinct we lose when we grow up.

NADIA: When you saw him, did you feel that thing from the soap operas, what the characters refer to as "the call of blood."

ALINA: Well, what I remember is his presence in my house, and he was a very tender and very pleasant man. Don't forget—he was also the hero of the moment.

NADIA: How did you take the news?

ALINA: I was ten years old, an emerging adolescent, so the news brought me relief, because I didn't have to keep saying my father was "a worm," a traitor. It didn't really surprise me; it relieved me, but I also knew it wasn't going to do me any good. It didn't change my life at all.

NADIA: From then on, after learning he was your father, did you see him more often? Did you talk about this among yourselves?

ALINA: He came, he visited frequently, but then he could disappear for a year.

NADIA: During your childhood he lived in Celia Sánchez's house. Did you ever meet her?

ALINA: Never. Not once.

NADIA: Was there ever a conversation between you that was transcendent, a cardinal conversation between you?

ALINA: No. By that time he was really into his monologues.

NADIA: Why don't you use his last name?

ALINA: When I was on the verge of adolescence, that relationship was more of a problem than a solution. First, a law had to be changed, and so the Family Code was passed. But by no means could you make that kind of name change in the fifties—that didn't happen in Cuba. By the time it was possible, I didn't want it, even though the law had been changed so I could.

NADIA: He changed it for you?

ALINA: Well, that's why he changed it. The person in charge of making the change was the minister of justice, Alfredo Yabur, but when it became possible, I didn't want it. Going to school and saying, "Don't call me this anymore, call me this," seemed ridiculous to me. Besides, I always remembered Dr. Orlando with great affection, because somehow I understood everything this man had suffered. He must have suffered a lot, a whole lot. Later, in time, I was able to resume, to reestablish my relationship with my sister, and I realized I'd been right.

NADIA: Knowing all this, did you feel you were being watched?

ALINA: I come from a family of matriarchs; my grandmother was such a beautiful woman that when she went to the theater, they put a spotlight on her. Naty was very beautiful too. If your mother took you to school in a Mercedes-Benz and your father came looking for you while wearing a linen uniform, you were already a freak, and I was always the freak.

NADIA: Were there ever bodyguards at the door during Fidel's visits?

ALINA: No, no, no, there were never bodyguards at the door. The only thing was when he came over there was always a great display of security. Then, well, people in the neighborhood found out, and they wanted to talk to him about the cousin who had been shot—all their tragedies. There was also that thing about "If you want, I can give him a letter" . . . I was always in the yard, and I read all those.

NADIA: How old were you then?

ALINA: Five. It all seemed surreal, because you have to be very desperate to give those kinds of letters to a five-year-old girl.

NADIA: You didn't use his last name because it was uncomfortable for you, but you were his only daughter . . . and the family, how did the family behave in the midst of such a strong presence? Did you sense any similarities?

ALINA: I'd have liked to be like my mother, who was a beautiful woman. My grandmother hated Fidel; she called him the devil. There was always a duality of emotions in the house. It has always been obvious to me that my mother loved him. When he came to visit her, there was a light in her eyes.

NADIA: Do you remember any special gift Fidel gave you?

ALINA: Well, I remember once, after he came back from the Soviet Union, he brought back a bear they'd given him, and he told me the bear was mine and I could visit the bear at any of his houses.

NADIA: A few more questions about your family, your father's side. You're the only girl in the family. Did you ever see your brothers as a child?

ALINA: I have two older brothers. I finally met them when I was eleven years old. At some point he told me I had another brother besides Fidelito. Then I went to see this other brother, just him. It was a very pleasant surprise. His mother was named Amalia and she was very much a housewife, very dedicated to her home, very humble. I loved going there. Fidel isn't that much into family; the one who is, is Raúl. I spent many weekends with him.

NADIA: So it was Raúl who took care of you?

ALINA: Not just me, all of us.

NADIA: Do you remember your cousins, Raúl's kids?

ALINA: How could I not remember them! I loved my oldest cousin—Deborah—so much. She was like a doll and had almost white hair. I used to look for her after school and then we'd leave together.

NADIA: Did you feel this was your family, Alina?

ALINA: Yes and no. Sometimes I slept with Vilma and Raúl when I stayed with them. I didn't want to go to Varadero for long, but I always had a place there with them. In different ways, I thought of them as family, not so much in other ways.

NADIA: Aren't you afraid of not belonging to anything?

ALINA: I've never belonged to anything, and that gives me a

lot of freedom. First of all, I'm a child out of wedlock—nowadays no one cares, but in the fifties that was a thing.

NADIA: Did you feel lonely or weird, humiliated?

ALINA: I must have felt lonely, weird, and humiliated, but that's just part of personal growth. And since there wasn't any structure back then, everything seemed normal.

NADIA: Do you remember your grandmother Lina, Fidel's mother?

ALINA: I only met my grandmother Lina two or three times, but I remember her at the naval hospital before she died. She was a woman with a lot of energy, and you had to ask, "How did this tiny woman produce this family of giants?"

NADIA: They named you Alina?

ALINA: It must have been my mother, because at that time Fidel was in Mexico.

NADIA: I think you didn't have issues with Fidel, the man who showed up at night, but you did with the man who ran the country. That began in your adolescence, right?

ALINA: Well, it was also about my mother's suffering and how he disappeared. I grew up without him . . . It never crossed my mind: "Oh, I have to call Fidel and tell him this or that." I didn't have his phone number; it had to be done through a third person. I think I realized very early he wasn't someone you could count on for anything. He wasn't going to explain my math homework to me because you can't do that at two in the morning.

NADIA: Did you call him Papi or Fidel?

ALINA: I called him Fidel.

NADIA: Do you call him Castro now?

ALINA: I call him Fidel.

NADIA: Let's say you had the normal tensions teenagers have

with their parents, but you couldn't discuss them with him, tell him about your suffering.

ALINA: I mostly suffered for my mother, who longed for recognition and social status. I'd have liked to have an ordinary father like everyone else, and grandparents and normal things, but none of that happened.

NADIA: Would you like to see him now, at the end of his life? Talk to him about all this?

ALINA: I'm convinced love is something that must be given in life, consciously, but that it's also a matter of habit, and I never had that due to the circumstances. Now, there's a rather exotic spiritual theory or belief that claims you choose the womb in which to come into life, so obviously it must be true I got myself into this trouble.

NADIA: When you had your daughter, how did you feel having her in your arms?

ALINA: I thought there must be something inherent in motherhood that is unconditional. I remember in delivery, apart from enormous relief, I considered the circumstances and the moment in which I'd brought this girl into the world. But she's never had any problems, so I consoled myself very quickly. Mumín is much more mature than I am. She was giving lessons in maturity from the moment she began to speak.

NADIA: Do you remember any stories about your daughter and Fidel?

ALINA: Well, we're talking about 1989, which was a year of reflection for many people, and which led to the fall of the Soviet empire, which had a very big impact on Cuba. The structural errors became evident, because when you stop being subsidized, the gaps appear, and they were deep.

At the time, I was friends with a foreign journalist. I'd tell him what was going on in my head. I was involved with the dissident movement. That Christmas, in 1989, a soldier showed up wanting to talk to my mother and not to me. I thought they wanted to prep my mother to raise my daughter because they were going to send me to one of those places where people are calm and quiet—and unable to discern—but that wasn't it. We were preparing for Armageddon, but that wasn't it either. According to this messenger, the comandante was concerned because his granddaughter was about to turn fifteen and he wanted to know what she wanted in order to send her a gift. It had nothing to do with my passionate political activism or with punishment.

NADIA: Did you expect punishment from him because you were defiant?

ALINA: Well, there are things he considers weaknesses and he rejects them, but that idea that exists in Cuba—that he's somehow implanted in us—that he's responsible for absolutely everything, is not really true. I believe if you're close to his loved ones, you're part of a strict surveillance because it's about taking care of his life, and that's a fact. I wasted a lot of time in my life trying to avoid that circumstance, but you can't really avoid it in any way.

NADIA: You have something to talk about with Fidel. Do you want resolution?

ALINA: No, I have resolution.

NADIA: Would you ever go back to Cuba?

ALINA: I had a really hard time there, especially the last few years, for many reasons. It's not a question of pressure, but eventually I'll return. Where else am I going to go? That's my country. I hope it's not because of a tragedy, really, because I've realized places don't get redeemed. There are people who say, "I'm going to go back to this place where I wasn't happy, but this time the place is going to give me an answer" . . . but it's not always like that.

NADIA: Could that be your fate?

ALINA: Fate has nothing to do with happiness. It's a task you take on. I imagine even European princes feel an enormous weight and some even abdicate. Well, I was the daughter of a Cuban prince, because at the beginning, that was his kingdom.

NADIA: So will you go back to say goodbye to your father?

ALINA: No, going back to say goodbye doesn't sound like a return.

NADIA: Would you redo your childhood?

ALINA: No, but I would rebuild my house, because it's falling apart.

AT THE NORTH OCEAN GRILL

I WALK alone in this city of no sidewalks. I look for areas where I can get places by myself. I try to get from one place to another, but I can do that only at the beach. I take notes about what's happening around me. Cuban phrases burst out and blow English away. Cuban music blasts through the walls. The smell of fried pork and black beans is very difficult to disguise. Cuban coffee, guava cakes, and a whole world unknown to me opens up at the Palacio de los Jugos, where the memorabilia of our food has made its home, food that's almost extinct on the island due to the endless crises.

I knew, from younger members of the family, that Chela, Celia's sister, couldn't grant me an interview because she'd lost her memory. Every family engagement drains her, and after a party, her memory had deteriorated considerably. She'd lost her son when the boy tried to go back to Cuba in a speedboat to attack the government. The boat was intercepted and blown up, and since then her health has been very fragile.

There's a concentration of pain in Miami, an intensity of what could have been, an obsession with nostalgia for what was lost. There's a certain sadness even when dancing. There's everything, but nothing tastes the same. Almost everyone's here, but no one's the same either. In Miami, our entire memory is a spare part. It's incredible to see that most of Celia Sánchez's family lives here, in the very heart of the "enemy."

The dark of the sea, the depth of the blackness, the humidity, and the heat reminded me of my nocturnal escapades to the beach at Santa María, or my perennial view of the Malecón. For a minute, I narrowed my eyes, and it seemed to me I was back in my usual place. But no. Time flies. I had only twenty-four hours left.

I could hardly sleep that night. "I want to know everything!" I went over what I'd talked about at the table with Celia's family. I hadn't been aware of a lot of it. I pondered: Are we happy where we choose to be? Is seeking happiness the right thing to do? The things I'd been told about my mother were not very different from what I already knew. That afternoon Arturo had called me. What he'd said about her made me think. "Your mother didn't love anyone; she couldn't because we didn't let her. We all fought over her love and left her empty." This will be good work, my literary effort, about the world in which Celia's, my mother's, and all the other women's contributions were erased in the name of the machismo Leninism instituted in Cuba.

FINAL PARTY IN MIAMI

CHONGO, THE youngest in Celia's family, suggests I have a party at his house with the people who were closest to Celia. There are so many things I still want to know; I accept his invitation because it'll be my last chance to talk to them. The apartment is spacious, glassed in, above the sea. You could jump off it like a diving board. The whole family came to say goodbye. I talked about some things with Acacia, and then, little by little, the brothers joined in.

I had taken the opportunity to invite some friends of my mother's too. I wanted to meet them. I had so many questions about my parents, issues I'm still processing; I don't know where they'll take me. Every Cuban is carrying a potential diary under their arm. Our lives are part of a book of silence we've been forced to write without words.

Acacia lent me her cell phone. I tried to call Lujo in Cuba, but it was impossible; the lines weren't working. I called Diego to tell him everything was in order. He'll be waiting for me tomorrow at the airport in Havana. We land at almost the same time. "I have so many things to tell you."

I invite my friends and my parents' friends. Arturo arrives at last, and when I open the door, I see we're wearing almost the same outfit.

I throw myself into his arms and we dance the night away. Arturo is very upset he had to abandon his career in

Cuba, his family, his previous life. I think this long distance is a feeling we all share, but there's no consolation, much less for me; I just feel more and more alone.

Arturo, who doesn't remember the Arturo of the '80s, when he danced at all the parties in Havana, was an exotic character who illuminated and inspired a huge group of artists. I adore him, and it's very hard for me to say goodbye. When will we meet again? Where? When I was a teenager I thought I'd live close to someone like him all my life, that nothing could separate us. We've had to let go of our loved ones; people who seemed eternal are far away today, lost, out of focus, with obsessions similar to our own. We've had to postpone what we most want—affection—on behalf of a society that's never understood or supported us.

Crazy and sensual, Arturo flew out of *Blade Runner* into Miami.

There was a great confusion in my head: interviews, words about my mother, questions about the history of Cuba, shops, dinners, purchases . . . I was going back more off-center than when I got here. Miami was much, much more complex than I had thought.

If I'd come to live here, who would I be today? Would I have married? Who? Would I have children? What would they look like?

I wonder if we'd married right, if our relationships made sense, if we'd created the unions we were supposed to. The Revolution had upset everything for its own sake. Our ties, here or there, were emergent, forged in times of war.

Suddenly the lights went down, everything went dark, and we started dancing to the Beatles, then Celia Cruz, and, finally, Los Van Van, with their usual chorus: *"Chirrín chirrán, chirrín chirrán que ya terminó, chirrín chirrán que ya no te quiero, chirrín chirrán te digo hasta luego, chirrín chirrán no, no, no."* Everything was spinning even though I hadn't had any wine. I wanted to be lucid to register it.

I was already drunk on Cuba and myself. We turned, dancing in the dark, changing partners and not knowing who was who. Hands on my waist, bodies against bodies, without distinction. In a rush, I thought about the conflicts my father always told me about between here and there. Between Miami and Cuba. Between Havana and its reflection. Now everything seemed to have stopped so we could dance: either there was a truce or the war was over, because everyone in the house was dancing, everyone in the house was singing. I felt happy knowing I wasn't outside this world, that I was well received here, and although I was passing through—because I hadn't come to stay—they didn't make me feel like an outsider. Part of me was with them, despite the fact that my home was waiting somewhere else, in front of the Malecón in Havana, on the curve of the seawall, where I'd return to at the end of this song and its *"chirrín chirrán,"* which was endless in my head.

I ran out of the party to pack. I didn't want to say goodbye; I'd rather say "See you tomorrow." Everything will seem like a dream once I'm back home. When will this absurd distance end? So close and yet so far.

JOURNEY TO HAVANA

We fly over the Florida Keys and see boats gliding on waves, people fishing. There's real life down there. The flight back is more relaxed, less tense.

When we spot Cuba, people who live in Miami crowd the windows. We fly past the Santa Cruz del Norte thermoelectric plant, over the oil wells and the fires. Lots of excitement, applause, shouts of joy.

They say: "It's Cuba, Cuba, Cuba." They sing "Guantanamera." They cry, walk up and down the aisles, hug each other. We haven't touched down yet, but according to them, we're already here. I look at the landscape and try to imagine what waits for me below: Diego, in his reporter outfit, asking about the future. Lujo at home with food ready and his endless questions about the past, and as a backdrop, the wet Malecón, because, from above, you can see it's about to rain.

The passenger next to me asks if I'm going to Cuba for the first time. I tell him I live in Havana. The flight attendant comes and asks him to sign a record for the pilot. She hands it over and continues on to the cabin. He's a sweet man, mulatto, short, serene, and friendly. He must be in his eighties. He tries to read what the cover of the record says, but he can't see very well and looks at me in dismay.

"Why do I have to sign this?"

I look at the record and realize he's Rubén González, one of the greatest Cuban pianists of all time. I lend him the pen with which I'm taking notes, but the man doesn't see the point of signing.

"Who's that?" he asks, looking at himself smiling on the cover.

"It's you. Will you sign the record for the pilot?"

"Yes, but who am I?"

"You're a great pianist, undoubtedly the best."

"Are you sure?"

"As sure as we're flying."

"Ah! But are we flying?" Rubén puts on his glasses, amazed by the record. He thought it wasn't real, and he looks at it as if for the first time. It's a double record, from a few years ago, but he doesn't remember it anymore.

"Did I play with them? Most of them have died, haven't they?"

"Some have," I say, a little nervous.

"And where am I now?"

"On a plane, going back to Cuba."

"Then we're neither here nor there. We're in the air."

I nod. He looks at the record again.

"You should sign it and maybe write a little something else first."

We are about to land and the passengers shout louder and louder. There is something ambiguous about it, something between laughter and tears. Finally, the elderly pianist signs the cover, just his name, moving a tremulous hand.

"Forgive me, young lady. Are we coming to or leaving Havana? I've been forgetting everything lately. I'm eighty years old. I hardly remember anything at the piano—just imagine."

"You were in Miami, but now we're landing in Havana."

The flight attendant serenely announces the details of the complicated arrival, then picks up the record, grateful for the gesture. She kisses the pianist, who doesn't understand anything, and hurries back to the cabin.

The plane hovers. It is raining hard in Havana. I see the lights of Cuba through a different prism, a leaden tone penetrated by the sun, diminishing to a surprising violet. I try on the idea that it's been ten years instead of four days since I've left, a good exercise in longing that doesn't work if you haven't lived far enough away. I feel I am falling onto the runway like onto a feather mattress, without the rigid ritual of landing, but we haven't touched ground yet. We circle around because the storm won't let us descend. Cuba is below, and we slowly enter the eye of the storm to make our way through the dark clouds.

The old pianist has fallen asleep. His hands play scales on the armrests. The passengers are silent now. We fly over the coast. Soon we are struck by a chilling void. The screams can't save us. We are still in the air, circling. The old pianist startles awake.

"What was I telling you?" he asks.

We hit the runway abruptly. It is pounding rain, and the passengers applaud. The old pianist undoes his seat belt, then shoots up to ceremoniously greet the applause around him. He looks down at me again.

"Where did you say we are?"

"In Havana," I say as I head toward the exit door, which is still closed.

WITHOUT FIDEL

Oh mother, oh mother. Air is a lightness that spins
around your head and becomes clearer when you laugh.

—*from* Nostalghia, *directed and co-written by Andrei
Tarkovsky, 1983*

HAVANA, NOVEMBER 25, 2016

The phone rings. I'm in the shower washing off the day's
sweat so I can go to bed. Cubans bathe at five o'clock, but
today I needed time to clean up the disaster left by the last
tourists and prepare the rooms for those coming to spend
New Year's Eve here.

What is Cuba to tourists?

Would I come to Cuba to spend New Year's Eve?

I don't know. I think for most people this place is still
a history museum. They find it curious, exciting; they walk
through the detritus of our lives, asking personal questions
as if they don't mind hurting us. Cuba is an unexplored
place; even I don't know what's happening on the other side

of the island. Time and time again I propose to go east, but I never leave Havana; I could never abandon it. Havana has a strange spell: it's watery, feminine, and sentimental, very difficult to quit.

The phone keeps ringing. My God, who could be insisting like that at this hour? I hope it's not a neighbor trying to get me to take in another tourist.

I try to ignore the ringing, but it's unbearable. It stops for an instant but immediately continues without remedy, rumbling around the arches in the house and tormenting me.

I leap wet from the tub onto the marble floor, slip, regain my balance, and grab the phone from next to the hair dryer.

It's Maruchi, a neighbor calling to tell me to turn on the TV, but she hangs up without explaining why.

I step into the hall and turn on the lights that lead to the living room, not worried about waking Lujo because he left for Miami today to look for stuff to decorate a new restaurant some Swedes are opening in Old Havana. If Lujo doesn't get out of here about once a month and breathe some fresh air, he'll die. Cuba suffocates everyone except me, who has learned to deeply love this confinement.

What's going on? I put on a nightgown and go out into the garden to find out. Cuban TV very rarely tells the truth, so I'd rather find out by just going outside.

A strange calm has taken over the Malecón. I look over at my neighbors' house, its doors and windows shuttered. I call Magda; she tries to say a few words, but the connection is terrible, even just to the house next door. I dial again, but an operator's voice says, "The lines are congested." I can tell from her tone that things are serious . . . I must turn on everything, everything, everything. I want lights, all the lights.

I flip on the TV, and Raúl is speaking to the people.

Fidel is dead.

I drape one of Lujo's coats—it had been hanging in the vestibule next to the hats—over my nightgown. I grab my wallet and lower the front windows a little, take my keys and go out to the streets.

The Malecón is deserted. Not a soul is out. I don't even see police watching over us. At the US Embassy there doesn't seem to be anything new to take care of or protect.

We've already been stripped of everything . . . What else can they take from us?

I walk against the wind. I cross El Vedado like a silk blade. My nightgown beats over my body and, looking like a sailing ship, I scale the hills into the dark. I'm getting thinner and weaker and looking more and more like my mother . . . The salty wind envelops me, this constant curse from the sea. The salt hits my face and clouds my vision. I can't see what's happening; the landscape is smoky and it seems like it will rain.

Where did everyone go?

As I walk my cell phone rings. It's Lujo from Miami.

"Hi," I say.

"*Maniiiiiiiiii, Manicero maniiiiiiiiiii.* He's goneeeeeeeeeee, he's gone."

"Yes, he's gone. It's over," I tell him.

"*Chirrín chirrán*, it's over now, *chirrín chirrán*, I don't love you anymore, *chirrín chirrán*, I'll see you later," Lujo sings.

"Are you having a good trip?" I ask, trying to make some sense in our crazy conversation.

"Yes, of course! But I can't believe this happened while I'm here. People in Miami are out on the streets. How is it over there? I'm worried about you, so lock yourself in and don't open the door for anyone, and don't rent to anyone until we see how this turns out," he begs me, now sounding desperate.

"There's nothing happening here. I'm walking on Línea. People are home. There's not a soul to be seen; the few of us who are out walking are silent," I explain patiently.

"But, Nadia, what are you doing out in the streets at this hour?" Lujo asks, a little upset. "What if something happens?"

"I'm going to Celia's house," I answer.

"Oh, for the love of God. Don't do that. Look—"

I cut him off and turn off the phone. I need to walk by myself, to follow my path without worrying. Fidel is dead. I don't need to follow any more orders.

When I get to Once Street, I realize the traffic light has been removed. There is no one at the guard post at Celia's house, no one watching the block.

I cross the stark avenue without fear. The truth is, I no longer care if anyone catches me. I was detained for three days when I tried to perform my book-play about Celia and her public persona. They took everything from my files, expelled Diego from Cuba for helping me reconstruct documents, and threatened Lujo with annulling his repatriation if he continued to help me search for the truth about this woman and her connection with Fidel.

Eight years have passed, and I haven't made art since: I don't write, I don't do anything other than rent rooms to tourists at my house in front of the Malecón.

I could have escaped like the rest of my contemporaries, the people with whom I studied, I think as I climb the stairs to Celia's building, but I don't want to become an exile. I can endure a search or an arrest, but to be an exile—I could never do that. I never liked what my mother became.

It's strange: this whole block was full of people Celia brought from Manzanillo or the Sierra to teach and live in Havana, people who were part of the revolutionary struggle but who now seem to have left the area. There's so much silence. People are still locked in their homes. Who will really care about this death? Will silence be a way of escape or an homage? Is it respect or fear that keeps them from taking to the streets?

I go up the stairs to Celia's house. There's a light on and the door is ajar, inviting me in. I hear Radio Reloj in the distance.

There's nothing left here, only the backdrop of what was once the archive of the Revolution.

I'm at peace. Nothing else can be taken from me, I say to myself so I can go in without fear. I have nothing, I expect nothing, I tell myself, breathing heavily.

I try to turn on more lights, but there really aren't any working fixtures. I step into her room; the landscape on the wall seems to have been blurred by humidity. I don't see the hammock or the acrylic armoire, nor her clothes or perfume bottles. The room with the gifts is empty; gone too are the boxes of documents she used to review on sleepless nights. In the kitchen it seems the stove hasn't been lit in months. I imagine her sitting on the stairs drinking coffee, talking to my mother in code so I wouldn't understand. There's nothing and no one here. In the office, the drawers are empty except for paperclips and old pencils, a thick dust covering the desk's glass top where Celia used to work. Maybe they transferred everything to the Council of State at the Plaza de la Revolucion.

When did Fidel stop coming to this house? Maybe when he had his first son with Dalia Soto del Valle? Did Dalia and Celia ever meet in person? Neither of them liked or were allowed the limelight. I think Celia was actually above all that. She was more than a woman to him; she was his conscience—he lost her too soon!

There's a musty smell so intense it makes me dizzy. It's the scent of ruins, waste, cat urine, and mold. I open a window and try to breathe, but everything's dead outside too. It's as if they've taken the guts out of the building and left only a shell floating in an anodyne block, its charm forsaken.

I climb up to the attic, where Fidel used to stay. I look down, and the swimming pool is empty. Everything seems to have been taken from his room. There are no sheets on the bed; the mattress leans against the wall, and its stains look like a map of Africa. A leak drips on some wild plants, and there's Havana below, shivering, gagged by clouds and silence.

What's happened here?

Who gave the order to loot everything? Maybe Raúl? Maybe Fidel himself?

How much of what was decided here could explain the puzzle behind this drama?

I go back the way I came. The ocher light from the stairway

leads me straight to the kitchen. I find the rudimentary coffee strainer Celia used, that thin canvas sleeve through which the hot water drains the flavor from the ground beans. I take it with me, in exchange for everything that's been taken from me. I want to keep it and make coffee with it, in her memory.

I return to the hallway, go down the stairs, and see there's an old man dozing with the radio on behind the door. Radio Reloj tells the time and takes us back to the *comandante en jefe*'s heroics.

"Have a good evening," says the only watchman alive, nodding between snores.

Once more I breathe in the salty air, and the damn wind pushes my body so that I barely manage to continue along the Malecón. I belong to that dynasty of women who go against the grain, trying to see things in a different way.

I close my eyes and I can see Celia and Mami going down the street that overlooks the FOCSA Building, the wind tossing their hair and nudging them so they can barely turn on M Street up to Twenty-Third, laughing like crazy, dead now. My silk gown seems to fly out from my body and toward the sea. I touch the silk and remember Celia's robes and my mother's very fine skin.

They say you never cry for just one reason; whether from anger or pain, tears flow for so many reasons. I want to cry, but not for Fidel, for them, for Mami and Celia. Why did they both die so young? Why has each and every writer I know who's had the courage to speak about this died too?

Today every Cuban has a different reason to cry; the shot's been fired into the sky and we don't know where to run, who to run from.

The warden's dead, the cage is open, but I don't feel an

urge to leave. Instead, I panic that a stranger will come through the door.

This silence is him slamming the door. How are we going to live now without someone telling us what to do?

Who will we ask for permission or forgiveness? How will we subsist without offering obedience?

A terrible idea crosses my mind as I put the key in the sea-rusted lock. Did they incinerate the memory of Celia?

I'm home and take off my coat, put down my wallet, and set some water on to boil.

I open the windows and look at the horizon, where, as always, no ship is coming to save us from what we've chosen. Who cares about Cuba? Only a few Cubans. I pour the coffee grounds into the small, thin canvas sleeve, press them down with a spoon, and slowly let the hot water filter through the soil, the coffee plantations.

It smells of Oriente province; it smells of Cuba. A crystal glass awaits the brew under the worn sleeve.

I believe at this time in this city I may be the only person concerned about memory; this is and will always be a country that prefers to forget.

I'm scared, I think, as I tip the glass of hot coffee into my mouth on my first daybreak without Fidel.

TRANSLATOR'S NOTE

Let me tell you about Cuban Spanish. It's a little different—and I don't just mean that we use words like *guagua* (a really great word) instead of *autobús*. Cuban Spanish is different because, first, it's pretty fast, especially in Havana. All that speed means things get left behind, like the *s* at the end of plurals; *l*'s might disappear in an inhalation, *d*'s can drop into deep, dark silent holes and are never heard from again.

Linguists talk about our weak pronunciation of consonants, about fricatives and the "debuccalization" of *s* in syllable coda. They rarely mention how Cubans end a lot of sentences with mouths open, or that a greater understanding of Cuban Spanish might come not just from the words themselves but from the gestures and presentation of the person who is speaking those words.

How, then, does this translate to the page? How do Cubans sound like Cubans when they're not being actively voiced but left to the singularity of the page?

Well, they sound like Wendy Guerra. On the page, Wendy doesn't necessarily drop the *s*'s or swallow the consonants, yet on the page, Wendy emblematizes *cubanidad*. Wendy is the voice of a generation of Cubans who came of age during the years of revolutionary glory and found themselves as adults in a world of dislocation and despair. The language Wendy uses harkens back to slogans and mantras, but she also infuses it with irony and bite. It's often indirect, dreamy, chock-full of song lyrics not just from the revolution but from romantic boleros and peasant songs, quotes from Dylan Thomas and Mexican novelists, it's cinematic and also incredibly intimate. It can be over the top. It can sometimes sound outrageous, especially when recalibrated into English.

Here's the thing for me about Wendy: she speaks my language; she writes my language. We're both Cuban-born but though she grew up in Cuba and I grew up in Indiana, both our families go back to a small village on the eastern side of the island called Banes and we share the particular inflections of that coastal area. She often reminds me that we're both children of Banes, women of Banes. And although it sounds a little hokey, I know what she means.

I know exactly what she means: we speak the same language.

I came to the US old enough to hold on to my mother tongue but also young enough to learn English as a native language. Wendy is curiously immune to English, but if that ever changed, I hope this is the English she'd be mouthing.

This is the third book of Wendy's I've translated, and in some ways the most challenging to translate. But as always, her Spanish puts me at ease—it feels like the most natural language in the world. I hope when you read it in English it feels that way to you as well.

Achy Obejas
Benicia, California
April 18, 2021

Here ends Wendy Guerra's
I Was Never the First Lady.

The first edition of this book was printed
and bound at LSC Communications in
Harrisonburg, Virginia, September 2021.

A NOTE ON THE TYPE

The text of this novel was set in Carré Noir Light,
a typeface designed by Albert Boton in 1996. A
native of France, Boton was working as a carpenter
at his father's workshop when, while installing new
windows in a city building, he discovered a graphic
design agency on the very last floor. Boton's encounter with the designers sparked his interest in
type, and he promptly left the workshop to strike
out on his own. After attending evening classes at
the École Estienne in Paris, Boton worked at several French design agencies of repute. In 1981, he
became the head of the type department at Carré
Noir, whose name inspired this elegant typeface.

HARPERVIA

An imprint dedicated to publishing international voices,
offering readers a chance to encounter other lives and other
points of view via the language of the imagination.